'So you're not expecting me to... to sleep with you...right away?'

He hooked one dark brow upwards. 'I thought you said you don't usually sleep with perfect strangers?'

She frowned at his tone, not sure if he was teasing her. 'Technically you're not a stranger, though, are you?' she said. 'I might not remember you, but there's enough evidence around to confirm we are married.'

A glint appeared in his dark-as-night gaze as it held hers. 'Are you inviting me to sleep with you, Emelia?'

Emelia felt her belly fold over itself. 'Er— no...not yet... I mean...no. No. It wouldn't be right for me or even fair to you.'

He came up close, lifting a portion of her hair, slowly twirling it around his finger until she felt the subtle tension on her scalp as he tethered her to him. 'We could do it to see if it unlocks your memory,' he said, in a voice that sounded rough and sexy. 'How about it, *querida*? Who knows? Perhaps it is just your mind th

will re

D0278211

Melanie Milburne says: 'I am married to a surgeon, Steve, and have two gorgeous sons, Paul and Phil. I live in Hobart, Tasmania, where I enjoy an active life as a long-distance runner and a nationally ranked top ten Master's swimmer. I also have a Master's Degree in Education, but my children totally turned me off the idea of teaching! When not running or swimming I write, and when I'm not doing all of the above I'm reading. And if someone could invent a way for me to read during a four-kilometre swim I'd be even happier!'

Recent titles by the same author:

CASTELLANO'S MISTRESS OF REVENGE
THE VENADICCI MARRIAGE VENGEANCE
BOUND BY THE MARCOLINI DIAMONDS

The Royal House of Karedes:

THE FUTURE KING'S LOVE-CHILD *(Book 6)*

Did you know that Melanie also writes for Medical™ Romance?

EMERGENCY DOCTOR AND CINDERELLA
THE DOCTOR'S REBEL KNIGHT

THE MÉLENDEZ FORGOTTEN MARRIAGE

BY
MELANIE MILBURNE

All the characters in this book have no existence outside the imagination of the author, and have no relation whatsoever to anyone bearing the same name or names. They are not even distantly inspired by any individual known or unknown to the author, and all the incidents are pure invention.

First published in Great Britain 2010
Harlequin Mills & Boon Limited,
Eton House, 18-24 Paradise Road, Richmond, Surrey TW9 1SR

© Melanie Milburne 2010

ISBN: 978 0 263 87816 5

Harlequin Mills & Boon policy is to use papers that are natural, renewable and recyclable products and made from wood grown in sustainable forests. The logging and manufacturing process conform to the legal environmental regulations of the country of origin.

Printed and bound in Spain
by Litografia Rosés, S.A., Barcelona

THE MÉLENDEZ FORGOTTEN MARRIAGE

To Gaile Donoghue,
a loyal and trusted friend for more years
than I can count. Thank you for your love and support.

Also, special thanks to Rebecca Fleming
and her grandmother, who were so helpful with
translating some words for me into Spanish. Thanks!

CHAPTER ONE

EVEN before Emelia opened her eyes she knew she was in hospital. At the blurred edges of her consciousness she vaguely registered the sound of shoes squeaking on polished linoleum and the swish of curtains and voices, both male and female, speaking in low hushed tones.

She half-opened her eyes. The light was bright, making her pupils shrink painfully. She squeezed her eyes shut and, after a moment or two, blinked again and, narrowing her still flinching gaze, looked at the nurse who was standing at the end of the bed with a chart in her hands.

'W-what happened?' Emelia asked, trying to lift herself upright in the bed. 'What am I doing here? What's going on?'

The nurse clipped the folder on the end of the bed before coming to lay a gentle hand on Emelia's shoulder to ease her back down. 'Mrs Mélendez, please don't upset yourself. You're in hospital. You had a car accident a week ago. You've been in a coma.'

Emelia felt her heart give a jerky beat in her chest like a kick. She frowned and then wished she hadn't as it made her head ache unbearably. She put a hand up to her forehead, her fingers encountering a thickly wadded bandage positioned there.

Hospital? Accident? Coma?

The words were foreign to her, but the most foreign of all was how the nurse had addressed her. 'W-what did you call me?' she asked, staring at the nurse with her heart still thudding out of time.

The nurse glanced over her shoulder as if looking for backup. 'Erm…I think I'd better get the doctor to explain,' she said and quickly bustled away.

Emelia felt as if she were trying to find her way through a thick fog while blindfolded. *Accident? What accident?* She looked down at her sheet and hospital blanket-covered body. Although she ached all over, she seemed to be in all one piece. No plaster casts were on any of her limbs so she obviously hadn't broken any bones. The worst pain was from her head, although she felt horrendously nauseous, but she assumed that was from the pain medication she had been given. She could see the drip leading from a vein in the back of her left hand where it was lying on the top of the bed. She quickly looked away as her stomach gave a rolling turn.

What had the nurse called her again… Mrs Mel… something or other? Her heart gave another little stutter. *Married?* Of course she wasn't married! There must be some mistake, a mix-up in the paperwork or something. They'd obviously got her name wrong. Her name was Emelia Louise Shelverton. She had moved abroad from Australia a couple of months ago. She lived in London, in Notting Hill. She worked part-time as a singer in The Silver Room at one of the top hotels a couple of blocks from Mayfair while she looked for a more permanent position as a music teacher.

Married? What a laugh. She wasn't even dating anyone.

'Ah, so you are finally awake.' A man who was clearly one of the senior doctors swished the curtains around Emelia's bed closed. 'That is very good news indeed. We've been quite worried about you, young lady.'

Emelia glanced at his name tag through eyes that were still slightly blurry. 'Dr…um…Pratchett? What am I doing in hospital? I don't know what's going on. I think there's been some sort of mistake. The nurse called me Mrs something or other but I'm not married.'

The doctor gave her a formal trust-me-I'm-a-doctor smile. 'You have suffered a head injury, Emelia,' he said. 'This has obviously caused you to have some memory loss. We don't know how extensive it is until we conduct further tests. I will have the staff psychologist assess you presently. We may also need to rescan you under MRI.'

Emelia put her hand to her head again, her brows coming together in a tight frown. 'I…I have amnesia?'

The doctor nodded. 'It seems so. Do you know what day it is?'

Emelia thought for a moment but knew she was only guessing when she offered, 'Friday?'

'It is Monday,' Dr Pratchett said. 'September tenth.'

Emelia drew in an uneven breath. 'What year is it?' she asked in a frightened whisper.

The doctor told her and she blinked at him in horror. 'That can't be right,' she said. 'I can't have forgotten two years of my life. That's ridiculous!'

Dr Pratchett placed his hand over hers where it was lying on the bed clutching the sheet in her fingers. 'Try to keep calm, Emelia,' he said soothingly. 'This is, of course, a very frightening and confusing time for you. You have been in a coma for several days so things will seem a little strange at first. But in time you may well remember everything. It just takes a little time. You need to take things very slowly at first. Baby steps, my dear. Baby steps.'

Emelia pulled her hand out from beneath the doctor's, holding it up like an exhibit at an investigation. 'Look,' she said, pushing her chin up. 'No rings. I told you—there's been some sort of mix-up. I'm not married.'

'You are very definitely Mrs Emelia Louise Mélendez,' the doctor assured her with authority. 'That is the name the police found on your driver's licence. Your husband is waiting outside to see you. He flew over from Spain as soon as he was informed of your accident. He has positively identified you as his wife. He has barely left your bedside the whole time you have been unconscious. He just stepped out a moment ago to take a phone call.'

Emelia's mouth fell open so wide she felt her chin drop almost to her chest. She felt her heart boom like a cannon exploding in her chest.

Her husband?

Her *Spanish* husband?

She didn't even know his Christian name. How could it be possible for her to forget something as important as that? Where had they met? When had they got married? Had they? How many times…?

Her stomach gave a funny little quiver… It wasn't possible…*was it*? How could she have lived with and loved a man and not remember him? Her skin broke out in a sweat, her palms hot and moist with uncertainty and fear. Was she dreaming? Surely she must be dreaming.

Think. Think. Think.

What was the last thing she had been doing? She scrunched her eyes closed and forced herself to concentrate but her head pounded sickeningly as she tried to recall the last few days. It was all a blur, a foggy indistinct blur that made little, if any, sense.

When Emelia opened her eyes the doctor had already moved through a gap in the curtains and a short time later they twitched aside again, the rattle of the rings holding the curtain on the rail sounding too loud inside her head.

She felt her breath stall in her throat.

A tall raven-haired stranger with coal-black deep set eyes stood at the end of the bed. There was nothing that was even vaguely familiar about him. She studied his face for endless seconds, her bruised brain struggling to place him. She didn't recognise any one of his dark, classically handsome features. Not his tanned, intelligent-looking forehead or his dark thick brows over amazingly bottomless eyes or that not short, not long raven-black hair that looked as if it had last been groomed with his fingers. She didn't recognise that prominent blade of a nose, and neither did she recognise that heavily shadowed jaw that looked as if it had an uncompromising set to it, and nor that mouth… Her belly gave another involuntary movement, like a mouse trying to scuttle over a highly polished floor. His mouth was sculptured; the top lip would have been described as slightly cruel if it hadn't been for the sensual fullness of his lower one. That was a mouth that knew how to kiss and to kiss to conquer, she thought, as her belly gave another little jiggle. She sent the tip of her tongue out to the sand dune of her lips. Had *she* been conquered by that mouth? If so, why couldn't she remember it?

'Emelia.'

Emelia felt her spine prickle at the way he said her name. His Spanish accent gave the four syllables an exotic allure, making every part of her acutely aware of him, even if she didn't know who the hell he was.

'Um… Hi…' What else was she supposed to say? *Hello, darling, how nice to see you again?*

She cleared her throat, her fingers beginning to pluck at the hem of the sheet pulled across her middle. 'Sorry…I'm a little confused right now…'

'It's quite all right.' He came to the side of her bed in a couple of strides, his tall presence all the more looming as he stood within touching distance, looking down at her with those inscrutable black eyes.

Emelia caught a whiff of his aftershave. It wasn't strong, but then he looked as if he hadn't shaved for a couple of days. There was a masculine urgency about the black stubble peppering his jaw, making her think of the potent male hormones surging through his body. She shakily breathed in another waft of his aftershave. The light fragrance had citrus undertones that smelt vaguely familiar. Her forehead creased as she tried to concentrate… Lemons…sun-warmed lemons…a hint of lime or was it lemon grass?

'The doctor said I can take you home as soon as you are well enough to travel,' the man said.

Emelia felt the skin on her back tingle all over again at the sound of his voice. It had such a sexy timbre, deep and low and unmistakably sensual. She could imagine him speaking in his native tongue; the musical cadences of Spanish had always delighted her. But there was something about his demeanour that alerted her to an undercurrent of tension. There was something about the unreachable depths of his eyes. There was something about the way he hadn't yet touched her. Not that she wanted him to…or did she?

She glanced at his long fingered tanned hands. They were hanging loosely by his sides—or was that a tight clench of his fingers he had just surreptitiously released?

Her eyes slowly moved up to meet his. Her chest tightened and her breathing halted. Was that anger she could see in that tiny flicker of a nerve pulsing by the side of his mouth?

No, of course it couldn't be anger. He was upset, that was what it was. He was obviously shocked to see her like this. What husband wouldn't be, especially if his own wife didn't even know who he was?

She moistened her lips again, trying to find a way out of the confusing labyrinthine maze of her mind. 'I'm sorry…you must think I'm terrible…but I don't even know…I mean…I…I…I don't remember your name…'

His top lip lifted in a movement that should have been a wry smile but somehow Emelia suspected it wasn't. 'I do not think you are terrible, Emelia,' he said. 'You have amnesia, *sí*? There is much you do not remember, but in time hopefully it will all come back to you. The doctor seems to think your memory loss will not be permanent.'

Emelia swallowed. What if it was? She had read a story a couple of years ago about a young woman who had lost her memory after a horrific attack. Her whole life had changed as a result. She hadn't even recognised her parents. Her brother and two sisters were total strangers to her.

'Perhaps I should introduce myself,' the man said, breaking through her tortured reverie. 'My name is Javier Mélendez. I am your husband. We have been married for almost two years.'

Emelia felt the cacophonous boom of her heart again. It felt as if her chest wall was going to blow open with the sheer force of it. She struggled to contain her composure, her fingers now clutching at the sheet of the bed either side of her body as if to anchor herself. 'M-married?' she choked. 'Truly? This is not a joke or something? We are legally married?'

He gave a single nod. 'It is our anniversary at the end of next month.'

Emelia had no hope of disguising her shock. She opened and closed her mouth, trying to get her voice to work. Her brain was flying off in all directions, confused, frightened, lost. How could this be? How could this man be her husband? How could her mind let her down in such a way? How could she forget her own wedding day? What cruel stroke of fate had erased it from her memory? She let out a breath that rattled through her lungs. 'Um…where did we meet?' she asked.

'We met at The Silver Room in London,' he said. 'You were playing one of my favourite songs as I walked in.'

Emelia ran her tongue over her lips again as part of the fog cleared in her head. 'I…I remember The Silver Room…' She put her hand to her aching eyes. 'I can picture it. The chandeliers…the piano…'

'Do you remember your employer?' Javier asked.

Emelia looked up at him again but his eyes were like glittering diamonds: hard and impenetrable.

'Peter Marshall…' she said after a moment, her spirits instantly lifting as the memories flooded back. At least she hadn't lost too much of her past, she thought in cautious relief. 'He manages the hotel. He's from Australia like me. I've known him since childhood. We went to neighbouring private schools. He gave me the job in the piano bar. He's been helping me find work as a private music teacher…'

Something flickered in his gaze, a quick lightning flash of something she couldn't quite identify. 'Do you remember why you came to London in the first place?' he asked in a voice that was toneless, showing no hint of emotion.

Emelia looked down at her hands for a moment. 'Yes…yes I do…' she said, returning her gaze to his. 'My father and I had a falling out. A big one. We have a rather difficult relationship, or at least we have had since my mother died. He married within a couple of months of her death. His new wife…the latest one? We didn't get on. Actually, I haven't got on with any of his wives. There have been four so far…' She lowered her gaze and sighed. 'It's complicated…'

'Yes,' he said. 'It always is.'

She brought her gaze back to his, searching his features for a moment. 'I guess if we're married I must have told you about it many times. How stubborn my father is.'

'Yes, you have,' he said, 'many times.'

Emelia pressed her fingers to the corners of her eyes, her frown still tight. 'Why can't I remember you?' she asked. 'I *should* be able to remember you.' *I need to be able to remember you, otherwise I will be living with a total stranger,* she thought in rising alarm.

His dark eyes gave nothing away. 'The doctor said you should not rush things, *querida*,' he said. 'You will remember when the time is right. It might take a few days or maybe even a few weeks.'

Emelia swallowed a tight knot of panic. 'But what if I don't?' she asked in a broken whisper. 'What if I never remember the last two years of my life?'

One of his broad shoulders rose and fell in a dismissive shrug that Emelia somehow felt wasn't quite representative of how he felt. 'Do not concern yourself with things that are out of your control,' he said. 'Perhaps when you are back at home at my villa in Seville you will remember bits and pieces.'

He waited a beat before continuing. 'You loved the villa. You said when I first took you there it was the most beautiful place you had ever seen.'

Emelia tried to picture it but her mind continued to be a blank. 'What was I doing in London?' she asked as soon as the thought popped into her head. 'You weren't with me in the car, were you?'

That lightning-quick movement came and went in his gaze again; it was like the hand of an illusionist making something disappear before the audience could see how it was done. 'No, I was not,' he said. 'You were with your—' he paused for a moment '—with Peter Marshall.'

Emelia felt a hand grab at her insides and twist them cruelly. 'Peter was with me?' Her heart gave a lurch against her breastbone. 'Was he injured? Is he all right? Can I see him? Where is he? How is he?'

The ensuing silence after her rapid fire of panicked questions seemed to contain a deep and low back beat, a slow steady rhythm that seemed to be building and building, leading Emelia inexorably to a disharmonious chord she didn't want to hear.

'I am sorry to be the one to inform you of this, but Marshall did not survive the accident,' Javier said again without any trace of emotion in his voice.

Emelia blinked at him in stunned shock. *Peter was dead?* Her mind couldn't process the information. It kept shrinking back from it, like a battered dog cowering out of reach of the next anticipated blow. *'No…'* The word came out hoarsely in a voice she didn't recognise as her own. 'No, that can't be. He can't be dead. He *can't* be… We had such plans…'

Javier's expression didn't change. Not even a flicker of a muscle in his jaw revealed an iota of what he was feeling. It was as if he were reading from a script for a role he had no intention of playing. His words were wooden, cool. 'He is dead, Emelia. The doctors couldn't save him.'

Emelia felt tears burst from her eyes, hot scalding tears that ran unchecked down her cheeks. 'But I loved him so much…' Her voice was barely audible. 'We've known each other for years. We grew up in the same suburb. He was such a supportive friend to me…' A thought hit her like a glancing blow and her eyes widened in horror. 'Oh, God…' she gulped. 'Who was driving? Did I kill him? Oh, God, God, God—'

He touched her then. His hand came down over hers on the bed just like the doctor's had done earlier, but his touch felt nothing like the cool, smooth professional hand of the *medico*'s. Javier's touch was like a scorching brand, a blistering heat that scored her flesh to the fragile bones of her hand as he pinned it beneath the strength of his. 'No, you did not kill him,' he said flatly. 'You were not driving. He was. He was speeding.'

Her relief was a minute consolation given the loss of a dear friend. *Peter was dead?* The three words whirled around and around in her head but she wouldn't allow them to settle. Maybe she was dreaming. Maybe this was nothing but a horrible nightmare. Maybe she would wake up any second and find herself lying in her sunny shoebox flat in Notting Hill, looking forward to meeting up with Peter later to discuss the programme for that night's performance, just as she did every night before taking her place at the grand piano.

Emelia looked down at her hand beneath the tanned weight of Javier Mélendez's. There was something about his touch that triggered something deep inside her body. Her blood recognised him even if her mind did not. She felt the flicker of it as it began to race in her veins, the rapid escalation of her pulse making her heart pound at the thought of him touching her elsewhere. *Had* he touched her elsewhere? Well, of course he must have if they were married…

She gave her head a little shake but it felt as if a jar of marbles had spilled inside. She groaned and put her free hand to her temple, confusion, despair, grief and disbelief all jostling for position.

Javier squeezed her hand with the gentlest of pressure but even so she felt the latent strength leashed there. 'I realise all this must be a terrible shock. There was no easy way of telling you.'

Emelia blinked away her tears, her throat feeling so dry she could barely swallow the fist-sized wad of sadness there. As if he had read her mind, he released her hand and pulled the bed table closer, before pouring her a glass of water and handing it to her.

'Here,' he said, holding the glass for her as if she were a small child. 'Drink this. It will make you feel better.'

Emelia was convinced nothing was ever going to make her feel better. How was a sip of water going to bring back her oldest friend? She frowned as she pushed the glass away once she had taken a token sip. 'I don't understand…' She raised her eyes to Javier's ink-black gaze. 'Why was I in London if I am supposedly married and living with you in…in Seville, did you say?'

His eyes moved away from hers as he set the water glass back on the table. 'Seville, yes,' he said. 'A few kilometres out. That is where I…where we live.'

Emelia heard the way he corrected himself and wondered if that was some sort of clue. She looked at his left hand and saw the gold band of a wedding ring nestled amongst the sprinkling of dark hairs of his long tanned finger. She felt another roller coaster dip inside her stomach and doing her best to ignore it, looked back up at him. 'If we are married as you say, then where are my rings?' she asked.

He reached inside his trouser pocket and took out two rings. She held her breath as he picked up her hand, slipping each of the rings on with ease. She looked at the brilliance of the princess cut diamond engagement ring and the matching wedding band with its glittering array of sparkling diamonds set right around the band. Surely something so beautiful, so incredibly expensive would trigger some sort of memory in her brain?

Nothing.

Nada.

Emelia raised her eyes back to his. 'So...I was in London...alone?'

His eyes were like shuttered windows. 'I was away on business in Moscow,' he said. 'I travel there a lot. You had travelled to London to...to shop.'

There it was again, she thought. A slight pause before he chose his words. 'Why didn't I go to Moscow with you?' she asked, frowning.

It was a moment before he answered. Emelia couldn't help feeling he was holding something back from her, something important.

'You did not always travel with me on my trips, particularly the foreign ones,' he finally answered. 'You preferred to spend time at home or in London. The shops were more familiar and you didn't have to worry about the language.'

Emelia bit her lip, her fingers plucking again at the sheet covering her. 'That's strange...I hate shopping. I can never find the right size and I don't like being pressured by the sales assistants.'

He didn't answer. He just stood there looking down at her with that expressionless face, making Emelia feel as if she had stepped into someone else's life, not her own. If she was deeply in love with him she would have gone with him, surely? What sort of wife was she to go off shopping—an activity she normally loathed—in another country instead of being by his side? It certainly didn't sound very devoted of her. More disturbing, it sounded a little bit like something her mother would have done while she was still alive.

After a long moment she forced herself to meet his gaze once more. 'Um...I know this might seem a strange question but—' she quickly licked her lips for courage before she continued '—were we…happily married?'

The question seemed to hang suspended in the air for a very long time.

Emelia's head began to ache unbearably as she tried to read his expression, to see if any slight movement of his lips, eyes or forehead would provide some clue to the state of the relationship they apparently shared.

Finally his lips stretched into a brief on-off smile that didn't involve his eyes. 'But of course, *cariño*,' he said. 'Why would we not be happy? We were only married for not quite two years, *sí*? That is not long enough to become bored or tired of each other.'

Emelia was so confused, so very bewildered. It was totally surreal to be lying here without any knowledge of her relationship with him. Surely this was the stuff of movies and fiction. Did this really happen to ordinary people like her? She began to fidget with the sheet again, desperate to be alone so she could think. 'I'm sorry but I'm very tired…'

He stepped back from the bed. 'It's all right,' he said. 'I have business to see to, in any case. I will leave you to rest.'

He was almost through the curtains when she found her voice again. 'Um…Javier?'

His long back seemed to stiffen momentarily before he turned to look at her. 'Yes, Emelia?'

Emelia searched his features once more, desperate to find some hook on which to hang her new, totally unfamiliar life. 'I'm sorry…so very sorry for not recognising you…' She bit her lip again, releasing it to add, 'If it was me in your place, I know I would be devastatingly hurt.'

His dark eyes seared hers for a beat or two before they fell away as he turned to leave. 'Forget about it, *querida*,' he said.

It was only after the curtains had whispered against each other as they closed did Emelia realise the irony of his parting words.

CHAPTER TWO

'WELL, today's the big day,' the cheery nurse on duty said brightly as she swished back the curtains of the private room windows where Emelia had spent the last few days after being moved out of the High Dependency Unit. 'You're finally going home with that gorgeous husband of yours. I tell you, my girl, I wouldn't mind changes places with you, that I wouldn't,' she added with a grin as she plucked the pillows off the bed in preparation for a linen change. 'If his looks weren't enough compensation, just think—I wouldn't have to work again, married to all that money.'

Emelia gave the nurse a tight smile as she tried to ignore the way her stomach nosedived at the mention of the tall, dark, brooding stranger who had faithfully visited her each day, saying little, smiling even less, touching her only if necessary, as if somehow sensing she wasn't ready for a return to their previous intimacy. To limit her interaction with him, she had mostly feigned sleep, but she knew once she went home with him she would have to face the reality of their relationship.

She had seen how the nurses practically swooned

when he came onto the ward each day. And this one called Bridget was not the only one to gently tease her about not recognising him. Everyone seemed reasonably confident her memory loss would be temporary, but Emelia couldn't help worrying about the missing pieces and how they would impact on her once she left the relative sanctuary of the hospital.

She had spoken to the staff psychologist about her misgivings and what she perceived was Javier's tension around her. Dr Carey had described how some partners found it hard to accept they were not recognised by the one they loved and that it would take a lot of time and patience on both sides to restore the relationship to what it had been before the accident. There could be anger and resentment and a host of other feelings that would have to be dealt with in time.

The psychologist had advised Emelia to take time to get to know her husband all over again. 'Things will be more natural between you once you are in familiar surroundings,' Dr Carey had assured her. 'Busy hospitals are not the most conducive environment to re-establish intimacy.'

Emelia thought about her future as she waited for Javier to collect her. She sat on the edge of the bed, trying not to think about the possibility of never remembering the last two years of her life. She had no memory of her first meeting with Javier, no memory of their first kiss, let alone their wedding day and what had followed. He had said she loved his villa but she couldn't even imagine what it looked like. She was being taken to live in a foreign country with a man who was a stranger to her in every way.

She ran her hands down her tanned and toned thighs.

She couldn't help noticing how slim she was now. Surely she hadn't lost that much weight during her coma? She had only been unconscious a week. She had struggled on and off with her weight for most of her life and yet now she was almost reed-thin. Her legs and arms were toned and her stomach had lost its annoying little pouch. It was flat and ridged with muscle she hadn't known she possessed.

Was this how Javier liked her to look? Had she adopted a gym bunny lifestyle to keep him attracted to her? How soon had she succumbed to his attentions? Had she made him wait or had she capitulated as soon as he had shown his interest in her? What had he seen in her? She knew she was blessed with reasonable looks but somehow, with his arrestingly handsome features and aristocratic bearing, he seemed the type who would prefer supermodel glamour and sophistication.

The police had come in earlier and interviewed her but she had not been able to tell them anything at all about the accident. It too was all a blank, a black hole in her memory that no attempt on her part could fill.

One of the constables had brought Emelia her handbag, retrieved from the accident, but even searching through it she felt as if it belonged to someone else. There was the usual collection of lip gloss and pens and tissues and gum, a frighteningly expensive atomizer of perfume and a sophisticated mobile phone that hadn't survived the impact. The screen was cracked and it refused to turn on.

She took out a packet of contraceptive pills and stared at the name on the box: *Emelia Mélendez*. There were only a couple of pills left in the press out card. She fingered the foil rectangle for a minute and then, without another thought, tossed it along with the packet in the rubbish bag taped to the edge of her bedside table.

Emelia placed her hand on her chest near her heart, trying to ease the pain of never seeing Peter again. That was a part of her life that was finished. She hadn't even been given the chance to say goodbye.

Javier schooled his features into blankness as he entered the private suite. *'Cariño,'* he said, 'I see you are all packed and ready to leave.'

He saw the flicker of uncertainty in her grey-blue gaze before she lowered it. 'There wasn't much to pack,' she said, slipping off the bed to stand upright.

He put out a hand to steady her but she moved out of his reach, as if his touch repelled her. He set his jaw, fighting back his fury. She didn't used to flinch from his touch. She used to be hungry for it. He thought of all the times he had taken her, quickly, passionately, slowly, sensually. She hadn't recoiled from his love-making until Marshall had come back on the scene. Javier's gut roiled with the thought of what she had got up to while his back was turned. How convenient for her to forget her perfidy now when the stakes had changed. The way she had received the news of Marshall's death confirmed her depth of feeling for him. She hadn't forgotten her lover and yet she had forgotten him—her legal husband.

Javier clenched his fingers around the handle of the small bag containing Emelia's belongings. A tiny flick knife of guilt nicked at him deep inside. He had to admit there were some things he hoped she wouldn't remember about their last heated argument. He had lost

control in a way that deeply ashamed him. Had his
actions during that ugly scene driven her into her lover's
arms? Or had she been planning to run away with
Marshall in any case?

What if she *never* remembered him?

No. He was not going to think about that possibility,
in spite of what the doctors and the psychologist had
said. He lived for the day when she would look at him
with full recognition in her grey-blue eyes. For the day
she would smile at him and offer her soft, full bee-
stung mouth for him to kiss; she would give him her
body to pleasure and be pleasured until every last
memory of her dead lover was obliterated.

And then and only then he would have his revenge.

'My car is waiting outside,' Javier said. 'I have a
private jet waiting for our departure.'

She gave him one of her bewildered looks. 'You…
you have a private jet?'

'*Sí*,' he answered. 'You are married to a very rich
man, *mi amor*, or have you forgotten that too?'

She bit into her bottom lip, her gaze falling away
from his as she continued walking by his side. 'Dr
Carey, the psychologist, told me some husbands find it
very hard to accept their wives don't remember them,'
she said. 'I know this must be hard for you. I know you
must feel angry and upset.'

You have no idea how angry, Javier thought as he led
the way out of the hospital. Anger was like a turbulent
flood inside him. His blood was surging with it, bulging
in his veins like red-hot lava until he felt he was going
to explode with it. How could he conceal the hatred he
felt for her at her betrayal? The papers were full of it
again this morning, as they had been for the past week.

Every headline seemed to say the same: the speculation about her affair with Marshall, their clandestine dirty little affair that had ended in tragedy. Javier knew he would have to work harder at controlling his emotions. This was not the time to avenge the past. What was the point? Emelia apparently had no recollection of it.

He cupped her elbow with the palm of his hand as he guided her into the waiting limousine. 'I am sorry, *querida*,' he said. 'I am still getting over the shock of almost losing you. Forgive me. I will try and be more considerate.'

She looked at him once he took the seat beside her, her eyes like luminescent pools. 'It's OK,' she said in a whisper-soft voice. 'I'm finding it hard too. I feel like I am living in someone else's body, living someone else's life.'

'It is your life,' Javier said. 'It is the one you chose for yourself.'

She frowned as she absently stroked her fingers over the butter-soft leather of the seat between them. 'How long did we date before we got married?'

'Not long.'

She turned her head to look at him. 'How long?'

'Six weeks.'

Her eyes went wide, like pond water spreading after a flood. 'I can't believe I got married so quickly,' she said, as if talking to herself. She shook her head but then winced as if it had hurt her. She lowered her gaze and tucked a strand of her honey-blonde hair back behind her ear, her tongue sweeping out over her lips, the action igniting a fire in his groin despite all of his attempts to ignore her physical allure. Sitting this close, he could smell the sweet vanilla fragrance of her skin. If he closed his eyes he could picture her writhing beneath him as he pounded into her, his body rocking with hers until they both exploded. He clenched his jaw and turned to look out of the window at the rain lashing down outside.

'Was it a white wedding?' she asked after a little silence.

Javier turned and looked at her. 'Yes, it was. There were over four hundred people there. It was called the wedding of the year. Perhaps if you see the photographs it will trigger something in your memory.'

'Perhaps…' She looked away and began chewing on her bottom lip, her brow furrowing once more.

Javier watched her in silence, mulling over what to tell her and what to leave well alone. The doctor had advised against pressuring her to remember. She was disoriented and still suffering from the blow of losing her lover. Apart from that first show of grief, she hadn't mentioned Peter Marshall again, but every now and then he saw the way her eyes would tear up and a stake would go through his heart all over again.

She suddenly turned and met his gaze. 'Do you have family?' she asked. 'Brothers or sisters and parents?'

'My mother died when I was very young,' he said. 'My father remarried after some years. I have a half-sister called Izabella.' He paused before adding, 'My father left Izabella's mother and after the divorce remarried once again. As predicted by just about everyone who knew him, it didn't work out and he was in the process of divorcing his third wife when he died.'

'I'm sorry for your loss,' she said quietly. 'Did I ever meet him?'

Javier stretched his lips into an embittered smile.

'No. My father and I were estranged at the time. I hadn't spoken to him for ten years.'

Her expression was empathetic. 'How very sad. How did the estrangement come about?'

He drew in a breath and released it slowly. 'My father was a stubborn man. He was hard in business and even harder in his personal life. It's why each of his marriages turned into war zones. He liked control. It irked him that I wanted to take charge of my own life. We exchanged a few heated words and that was it. We never spoke to each other again.'

Emelia studied his stony expression, wondering how far the apple had fallen from the tree. 'Were you alike in looks?' she asked.

His eyes met hers, so dark and mysterious, making her stomach give a little unexpected flutter. 'We shared the same colouring but had little else in common,' he said. 'I was closer to my mother.'

'How old were you when she died?' Emelia asked.

His eyes moved away from hers, his voice when he spoke flat and emotionless. 'I was four, almost five years old.'

Emelia felt her insides clench at the thought of him as a dark-haired, dark-eyed little boy losing his mother so young. She knew the devastation so well. She had been in her early teens when her mother had died, but still it had hit hard. Her adolescence, from fourteen years old, had been so lonely. While not particularly close to either of her high-flying parents, there had been so many times over the years when Emelia had wished she could have had just one more day with her mother. 'Are you close to your half-sister?' she asked.

His lips moved in a brief, indulgent-looking smile

which immediately softened his features, bringing warmth into his eyes. 'Yes, strangely enough. She's a lot younger, of course. She's only just out of her teens but, since my father died, I've taken a more active role in her life. She lives in Paris with her mother but she comes to stay quite regularly.'

'So...I've met her, then?' Emelia asked, trying to ignore the way her stomach shifted in response to his warmer expression.

His eyes came back to hers, studying her for a pulsing moment. 'Yes,' he said. 'You've met her numerous times.'

Emelia moistened her lips, something she seemed to do a lot around him. 'Do we...get on?' she asked, choosing her words carefully.

His unreadable gaze bored into hers. 'Unfortunately, you were not the best of friends. I think it was perhaps because Izabella was used to having my undivided attention. She saw you as a threat, as competition.'

She frowned as she thought about what he had said about his sister. The girl sounded like a spoilt brat, too used to having her own way. No wonder they hadn't got on. 'You said Izabella was used to having you to herself. But surely you'd had women in your life before...before me?'

'But of course.'

Emelia felt a quick dart of jealousy spike her at the arrogant confidence of his statement. Just how many women *had* there been? Not counting him, for she could not recall sleeping with him, she had only had one lover. She had been far too young and had only gone out with the man to annoy her father during one of her teenage fits of rebellion. It was not a period of her life she was particularly proud of and the loss of self-esteem she had experienced during that difficult time had made it hard for her to date with any confidence subsequently.

Her belly gave another little quiver as she thought about what Javier might have taught her in the last two years. Had he tutored her in the carnal delights he seemed to have enjoyed so freely?

His dark eyes began to glint as if he could read her mind. 'We were good together, Emelia,' he said. 'Very, very good.'

She swallowed tightly. 'Um…I…it's…I don't think I'm ready to rush into…you know…picking up where we left off, so to speak.'

He elevated one of his dark brows. 'No?'

Emelia pressed her trembling thighs together, the heat that had pooled between them both surprising and shocking her. 'The doctor said not to rush things. He said I should take things very slowly.'

The little gleam in his eyes was still there as he held her gaze. 'It would not do to go against doctor's orders, now, would it?'

She couldn't stop herself from looking at his mouth. The sensual curve of his lips made her heart start to race. How many times had that mouth sealed hers? Was he a hard kisser or soft? Fast and furious with passion or slow and bone-meltingly commanding? The base of her spine gave a shivery tremor, the sensation moving all the way up to nestle in the fine hairs on the back of her neck.

Her thoughts went racing off again.

Had he kissed her *there*? Had he stroked his long tanned fingers over the nape of her neck? Had he dipped his tongue into the shell of her ear?

Her heart rammed against her ribcage.

Had he gone lower to the secret heart of her? Had he explored her in intimate detail, making her flesh quiver and spasm in delight? What positions had they made love in? Which was their favourite? Had she taken him in her mouth; had she…? Oh, God, *had* she…?

She sneaked a quick glance at him, her face flaming when she encountered his unknowable eyes.

He lifted his hand and with a barely there touch tracked the tip of one of his fingers over the curve of her warm cheek. 'You don't remember anything, do you, *querida*?' he asked in a husky tone.

Emelia pressed her lips together in an effort to stop them from prickling with sensation, with an aching burning need. 'No…no… I'm sorry…'

He gave her a crooked smile that didn't quite make the full distance to his eyes. 'It is no matter. We can take our time and do it all again, step by step. It will be like the first time again, *sí*?'

Emelia felt her heart start to flap as if it had suddenly grown wings. 'I wasn't very experienced…I remember that. I'd only had one lover.'

'You were a fast learner.' His eyes dipped to her mouth, lingering there for a moment before coming back to her eyes. 'Very, very fast.'

She swallowed again to clear the tightness of her throat. 'You must find this rather…unsettling to be married to someone who doesn't even remember how you kiss.'

His fingers went to her chin, propping her face up so she had to lock gazes with him. 'You know, I could clear up that little mystery for you right here and now.'

She tried to pull back but he must have anticipated

it as his fingers subtly tightened. 'I…I wasn't suggest-ing…' she began.

'No, but I was.'

Emelia felt her skin pop up in goosebumps as he angled his head and slowly brought his mouth within touching distance of hers. She felt the warm breeze of his breath waft over her lips, a feather-light caress that made her mouth tingle with anticipation for more. She waited, her eyes half closed, her heart thudding in ex-pectation as each second passed, throbbing with tension.

His fingers left her chin to splay across her cheeks, his thumbs moving back and forth in a mesmerising motion, his eyes heavy-lidded as they focused on her mouth. She sent her tongue out to moisten her lips, her heart giving another tripping beat as his mouth came just that little bit closer…

'It might complicate things for you if I kiss you right now,' he said in a rumbling deep tone. 'It wouldn't do to compromise your recovery, now would it, *cariño*?'

'Um…I…I…It's probably not a good idea right now…'

He gave a low deep chuckle and released her, sitting back in his seat with indolent grace. 'No,' he said. 'I thought not. But it can wait. For a while.'

Emelia sat in silence, trying to imagine what it was like for him. Of course he would find this situation un-bearably frustrating. He was a full-blooded healthy male in the prime of his life. And for the last two years he had been used to having her as his willing wife. Now she was like a stranger to him and him to her. Would her reticence propel him into another woman's arms? The thought was strangely disturbing. Why would the thought of him seeking pleasure in another woman's arms make her feel so on edge and irritable? It wasn't as if she had any memory of their time together.

Emelia looked down at the rings on her finger. It was strange but the weight of them was not as unfamiliar as the man who had placed them there. She turned them around; they were loose on her but she had lost even more weight from being in hospital. She hadn't noticed it earlier but she had a slight tan mark where the rings had been, which put to rest any lingering doubts about the veracity of their marriage. She glanced at him and found him watching her with a brooding set to his features. 'Is everything all right?' she asked.

'Of course,' he said. 'I just hope the flight will not be too tiring for you.'

He leaned forward to say something to the driver. Emelia felt the brush of his thigh against hers and her heart stopped and started at the thought of how many times those long strong legs had been entwined with hers in passion. He had held off from kissing her but how long before he decided to resume their physical relationship in full? She squeezed her thighs together again, wondering if she could feel where he had been; might it have been only just over a week ago?

They boarded the private jet after going through customs. She couldn't remember flying on a private Gulfstream jet before. She couldn't recall even seeing one other than in a magazine. Even her father, as wealthy as he was, always used a commercial plane, albeit business or first class. Had travelling in such opulent luxury and wearing diamonds that were priceless become commonplace to her in the last two years?

Even though Emelia could see her married name on

her passport, it still seemed as if someone had stolen her identity. The stamps on her passport made no sense to her. She had been to Paris, Rome, Prague, Monte Carlo and Zurich and London numerous times yet she remembered nothing of those trips.

The jet was luxuriously appointed, showcasing the wealth Javier had alluded to earlier. He was clearly a man who had made his way in the world in a big way. The staff members were all very respectful and, unlike some of the wealthy men Emelia had met amongst her father's set, Javier treated them with equal respect. He addressed each of them by name and asked after their partners and family as if they were as important to him as his own.

'Would you like today's papers?' one of the flight attendants asked once they were settled in their seats.

'Not today, thank you, Anya,' Javier said with a ghost of a rueful smile.

Emelia suppressed a little frown of annoyance. She would have liked to have read up on the news. After all, it was a different world she lived in now. She had two years' worth of news and gossip to catch up on. And then another thought came to her. Maybe there was something about the accident in the papers, some clue as to what had caused it. Peter, as the manager of a trendy hotel, well frequented by the jet-setting crowd of London, had been a popular public figure. Surely she had a right to know what had led up to the tragic accident that had taken her friend from her.

'Don't pout, *querida*,' Javier said when he caught the tail end of her look. 'I am trying to protect you.'

Emelia frowned at him. 'From what?' she asked.

He gave her one of his unreadable looks. 'I think you

should know there has been some speculation about your accident,' he said.

Her frown deepened. 'What sort of speculation?'

'The usual gossip and innuendo the press like to stir up from time to time,' he said. 'You are the wife of a high profile businessman, Emelia. You might not remember it, but you were regularly hounded by the press for any hint of a scandal. It's what sells papers and magazines, even if the stuff they print isn't always true.'

Emelia chewed on the end of one of her neatly manicured nails. *She* was the focus of the press? How could that be possible? She lived a fairly boring life, or at least she thought she had until after she had woken up from her coma. She had long ago given up her dreams of being a concert pianist and was now concentrating on a career in teaching. But the sort of fame or infamy Javier was talking about had definitely not been a part of her plan.

She dropped her finger from her mouth. 'What are the papers saying about the accident?' she asked.

His dark eyes hardened as they held hers. 'They are saying you were running away with Peter Marshall.'

Emelia opened her eyes wide. 'Running away? As in…as in leaving you?'

'It is just gossip, Emelia,' he said. 'Such things have been said before and no doubt they will be said again. I have to defend myself against similar claims all the time.'

She pressed her lips together. 'I might not be able to remember the last two years of my life but I can assure you I'm not the sort of person to run away with another man whilst married to another,' she said. 'Surely you don't believe any of that stuff?'

He gave her a slight movement of his lips, not exactly a smile, more of a grimace of resignation. 'It is the life we live, *querida*. All high profile people and celebrities are exposed to it. It's the tall poppy syndrome. I did warn you when we met how it would be. I have had to live with it for many years—lies, conjecture, gossip, innuendo. It is the price one pays for being successful.'

Emelia gnawed on her fingernail again as the jet took off from the runway. She didn't like the thought of people deliberately besmirching her name and reputation. She wasn't a cheater. She believed in absolute faithfulness. She had seen first-hand the damage wrought when a partner strayed, as her father had played around on each of his wives, causing so much hurt and distress and the betrayal of trust.

'Do not trouble yourself about it for now,' Javier said into the silence. 'I wouldn't have mentioned the press except they might be waiting for us when we arrive in Spain. I have made arrangements with my security team to provide a decoy but, just in case, do not respond to any of the press's questions, even if they are blatantly untrue or deliberately provocative. Do you understand?'

Emelia felt another frown tug at her brow. 'If they are as intrusive and persistent as you say, I can't evade the press for ever, though, can I?' she asked.

His eyes were determined as they tethered hers. 'For the time being, Emelia, you will do as I say. I am your husband. Please try to remember that, if nothing else.'

Emelia felt a tiny worm of anger spiral its way up her spine. She squared her shoulders, sending him a defiant glare. 'I don't know what you expected in a wife when you married me, but I am not a doormat and I don't intend to be one, with or without the possession of my memory.'

A muscle clenched like a fist in his jaw, and his eyes became so dark she couldn't make out where his pupils began and ended. 'Do not pick fights you have no hope of winning, Emelia,' he said in a clipped tone. 'You are vulnerable and weak from your injury. I don't want you to be put under any more pressure than is necessary. I am merely following the doctor's orders. It would help if you would do so too.'

She folded her arms tightly beneath her breasts. 'Do not speak to me as if I am a child. I know I am a little lost at present, but it doesn't mean I've completely lost my mind or my will.'

Something about his expression told Emelia he was fighting down his temper with an effort. His mouth was flat and white-tipped and his hands resting on his thighs were digging into the fabric of his trousers until his knuckles became white through his tan.

It seemed a decade until he spoke.

'I am sorry, *cariño*,' he said in a low, deep tone. 'Forgive me. I am forgetting what an ordeal you have been through. This is not the time to be arguing like an old married couple.'

Emelia shifted her lips from side to side for a moment, finally blowing out her cheeks on a sigh. 'I'm sorry too,' she said. 'I guess I'm just not myself right now.'

'No,' he said with an attempt at a smile. 'You are certainly not.'

She closed her eyes and, even though she had intended to feign sleep, in the end she must have dozed off as when she opened her eyes Javier was bringing his airbed seat upright and suggested she do the same, offering her his assistance as she did so.

Within a short time they were ushered through customs and into a waiting vehicle with luckily no sign of the press Javier had warned her about.

The Spanish driver exchanged a few words with Javier which Emelia listened to with a little jolt of surprise. She could speak and understand Spanish? She hadn't spoken it before coming to London. Had she learned in the last couple of years? Why, if she could remember his language, could she not remember the man who had taught it to her? She listened to the brief exchange and, for some reason she couldn't quite explain, she didn't let on that she understood what was being said.

'*Ella se acuerda algo?*' the driver asked. *Does she remember anything?*

'*No, ninguno,*' Javier responded heavily. Not a thing.

During the drive to the villa Emelia looked out at the passing scenery, hoping for a trigger for her memory, but it was like looking at a place for the first time. She felt Javier's gaze resting on her from time to time, as if he too was hoping for a breakthrough. The pressure to remember was all the more burdensome with the under-current of tension she could feel running beneath the surface of their tentative relationship. She kept reassuring herself it was as the doctors had said: that Javier would find it difficult to accept she couldn't remember him, but somehow she felt there was more to it than that. Even the driver's occasional glances at her made her feel as if she were under a microscope. Was it always going to be like this? How would she bear it?

When the car purred through a set of huge wrought iron gates, Emelia felt her breath hitch in her throat. The villa that came into view as they traversed the tree-lined driveway was nothing if not breathtaking. Built on four levels with expansive gardens all around, it truly was everything a rich man's castle should be: private, imposing, luxurious and no expense spared on keeping it that way. Even from the car, Emelia could see a team of gardeners at work in the grounds and, as soon as the driver opened the car door for her and Javier, the massive front doors of the villa opened and a woman dressed in a black and white uniform waited at the top of the steps to greet them.

'*Bienvenido a casa, señor.*' The woman turned and gave Emelia a haughty look, acknowledging her through tight lips. '*Señora. Bienvenido a casa.*'

'Thank you,' Emelia said with a strained smile. 'It is nice to be…er…home.'

'*Querida.*' Javier put his hand in the small of Emelia's back. 'This is Aldana,' he said. 'She keeps the villa running smoothly for us. Don't worry. I have explained to all of the staff that you will not remember any of them.'

'I'm so sorry,' Emelia said to Aldana. 'I hope you are not offended.'

Aldana folded her arms across her generous bosom, her dark sparrow-like eyes assessing Emelia in one sweeping up and down look. 'It is no matter,' she said.

'I will take Emelia upstairs, Aldana,' Javier said and, switching to Spanish, asked, 'Did you do as I asked when I phoned?'

Aldana gave a nod. '*Sí, señor.* All is back where you wanted it.'

Emelia continued to pretend she hadn't understood what was being said but she couldn't help wondering what exactly Javier had asked the housekeeper to do.

Her lower back was still burning where his hand was resting. She could feel each and every long finger against her flesh; even the barrier of her lightweight clothes was unable to dull the electric sensation of his touch. Her body tingled from head to foot every time she thought of those hands moving over her, stroking her, caressing her, touching her as any normal loving husband touched a wife he loved and desired.

When he led her towards the sweeping grand staircase she felt the wings of panic start to flap inside her with each step that took her upwards with him.

Even though he was nothing but a stranger to her would he expect her to share his bedroom?

His bathroom?

Or, even more terrifying…his bed?

CHAPTER THREE

'TRY not to be too upset by Aldana's coldness,' Javier said as they came to the first landing. 'It means nothing. She will get over it in a day or so. She was like that the first time I brought you home with me after we were married. She thought I was making the biggest mistake of my life, not just by marrying a foreigner, but by marrying within weeks of meeting you.'

Emelia suppressed a frown as she continued with him up the stairs. She had seen undiluted hatred in the housekeeper's eyes. How long had that been going on? Surely not for the whole time they had been married? How had she coped with such hostility? It surely wouldn't have made for a very happy home with a household of staff sending dagger looks at every opportunity.

She put her hand on the banister to steady herself after the climb. Her legs felt weak and her chest tight, as if she had run a marathon at high altitude.

'Are you all right?' he asked, taking her free hand in his.

She gave him a weak smile. 'Just a little light-headed... It'll pass in a moment.'

Emelia felt his fingers tighten momentarily on hers, the itchy little tingles his touch evoked making her feel even more dazed than the effort of climbing the staircase. His eyes were locked on hers, penetrating, searing, all-seeing, but showing nothing in return. 'Did your housekeeper eventually come to approve of your choice of wife?' she asked.

He released her hand, his eyes moving away from hers. 'I do not need the approval of my housekeeper, Emelia,' he said. 'We are married and that is that. It is no one's business but our own.'

Emelia's teeth sank into her bottom lip as she trudged up the rest of the stairs. She looked for signs of her previous life in the villa but there was nothing to show her she had lived here for close to two years. The walls were hung with priceless works of art; as far as she could see, there were no photographs of their life together. The décor was formal, not relaxed and welcoming. It spoke of wealth and prestige, not family life and friendliness. She could see nothing of herself in the villa, no expression of her personality and taste, and wondered why.

Javier opened a door further along the hall that led into a master bedroom of massive proportions. 'This was our room,' he said.

Emelia wasn't sure if he spoke in the past tense to communicate he would no longer be sharing it with her and she was too embarrassed to ask him to clarify. 'It's very big…'

'Do you recognise anything?' he asked as he followed her into the suite.

Emelia looked at the huge bed and tried to imagine herself lying there with Javier's long strong body beside her. Her stomach did a little flip-flop movement and she shifted her gaze to the bedside tables instead. On one side there was a wedding photograph and she walked over and slowly picked it up, holding her breath as she looked at the picture of herself smiling with Javier standing by her side.

She wrinkled her brow in concentration. Surely there was somewhere in her mind where she could locate that memory. The dress she was wearing was a dream of a wedding gown, voluminous and delicately se-quinned all over with crystals. She could only imagine how much it must have cost. The veil was at least five metres long and had a tiara headpiece, making her look like a princess. The bouquet of orange blossom she carried and the perfection of her hair and make-up spoke of a wedding day that had been meticulously planned. It looked like some of the society weddings she had been forced to attend back at home with her father. All show and fuss to impress others, crowds of people who in a year or so would not even remember the bride's and groom's names. She loathed that sort of scene and had always sworn she would not be a part of it when or if she married. But, as far as she could tell from the photograph in her hands, she had gone for shallow and showy after all.

She shifted her concentration to Javier's image. He was dressed in a dark suit and a white shirt and silver and black striped tie that highlighted his colouring and his tall commanding air. His smile was not as wide as Emelia's; it seemed a little forced, in fact. She wondered if she had noticed it on the day and been worried about it or whether she had been too caught up in being the centre of attention.

Emelia looked up from the photograph she was holding to see Javier's watchful gaze centred on her. 'I'm sorry…' She placed it back on the bedside table with a hand that was not quite steady. 'I can't remember anything. It's as if it happened to someone else.'

His dark gaze dropped to the image of them in their wedding finery. 'Sometimes when I look at that photograph, I think the very same thing,' he said, the slant of his mouth cryptic.

Emelia studied him for a moment in silence. Was he implying he had come to regret their hasty marriage? What had led him to offer her marriage in the first place? So many men these days shied away from the formal tie of matrimony, choosing the less binding arrangement of living together or, even more casually, moving between two separate abodes, thus maintaining a higher level of independence.

Had those first two years of marriage taken the shine off the passion that had apparently brought them together? Relationships required a lot of hard work; she knew that from watching her father ruin one relationship after another with no attempt on his part to learn from his previous mistakes. Had Javier fallen out of love with her? He certainly didn't look like a man in love. She had seen desire in his eyes, but as for the warmth of lifelong love…well, would she recognise it even if she saw it?

Javier caught her staring at him and raised one brow. 'Is something wrong, Emelia?'

She moistened her lips, trying not to be put off by the dark intensity of his gaze as it held hers. 'Um…I was wondering why you wanted to get married so quickly. Most of the men I know would have taken years to propose marriage. Why did you decide we should get married so quickly?'

There was a movement deep within his eyes, like a rapid-fire shuffle of a deck of cards. 'Why do you think?' he said evenly. 'Do you think you were not in the least agreeable to being married to me? I can assure you I did not have to resort to force. You accepted my proposal quite willingly.'

Emelia gave a little shrug, trying not to be put off by the black marble of his gaze as it held hers. 'I don't know…I guess it's just that I don't remember being on the hunt for a husband or anything. I'm only twenty-five—'

'Twenty-seven,' he corrected her.

Emelia chewed at her lip. 'Ri-ght…twenty-seven…' She lowered her gaze and frowned.

He tipped up her face with one finger beneath her chin. 'I wanted you from the moment I saw you sitting at that piano,' he said. 'It was an instant attraction. You felt it too. There seemed no point in delaying what we both wanted.'

Emelia looked into the blackness of his eyes and felt the tug of attraction deep and low in her body. Was this how it had been? The magnetic pull of desire, an unstoppable force that consumed every bit of common sense she possessed? She felt the burn of his touch; the nerve endings beneath her skin were jumping and dancing where his fingertip rested. 'How soon did we—' she swallowed tightly '—sleep together?'

He brushed the pad of his thumb across her bottom lip. 'How soon do you think?' he asked in a low, smoky tone.

Emelia felt the deep thud of her heart as his strong

thighs brushed against hers. 'I...I'm not the type to jump into bed with someone on the first date.'

His dark eyes glinted. 'You sound rather certain about that.'

Her eyes widened in shock. 'Surely I didn't...?'

He dropped his hand from her face. 'No, you didn't,' he said. 'I was impressed by your standards, actually. You were the first woman I had ever dated who said no.'

Emelia gave herself a mental pat on the back. He would be a hard one to say no to, she imagined. 'Did that make me a challenge you wanted to conquer?' she asked.

He gave her an enigmatic smile. 'Not for the reasons you think.'

Her gaze went to the wedding photograph again. 'I don't suppose we waited until the wedding night.'

'No.'

Emelia wondered how one short word could have such a powerful effect on her. Her skin lifted all over at the thought of him possessing her. Her breasts prickled with sensation, her belly flapped like washing on a line in a hurricane and her heart raced. But all she had was her imagination. Her mind was empty, a total blank. She felt cheated. She felt lost and afraid she might never be able to reclaim what should have been some of the most memorable days of her life. She gave a little sigh and faced him again. 'The funny thing is there are some people—like my father, for instance—who would give anything to forget their wedding days. But I can't recall a thing...n-not a thing...' Her voice cracked and she placed her head in her hands, embarrassed at losing control of her emotions in front of him.

He placed a gentle hand on her shoulder. 'Don't cry, *querida*,' he said.

His low soothing tone was her undoing. She choked on another sob and stumbled forward into the rock-hard wall of his chest. Her arms automatically wound around his lean waist, her face pressing into his shirt front, breathing in his warm male scent. Her body seemed to fit against him as if fashioned exactly to his specifications. She felt the strong cradle of his pelvis supporting hers, his muscled thighs holding her trembling ones steady. Her body tingled with awareness as she felt the swelling of his groin against her. How many times had he held her like this? She felt the flutter of her pulse in response, the tight ache between her thighs that felt both strange and familiar.

One of his hands went to the back of her head and began stroking her in a gentle, rhythmic motion, his voice when he spoke reverberating against her ear, reminding her of the deep bass of organ pipes being softly played in a cavernous cathedral. 'Shh, *mi amor*. Do not upset yourself. Do not cry. It can't change anything.'

Emelia tried to control her trembling bottom lip as she eased back to look up at him. 'I want to remember. I want to remember everything. What girl can't remember her wedding day? How can I live my life with whole chunks of it missing?'

Javier brushed her hair back from her face, his dark steady eyes holding her tear-washed ones. 'There are no doubt other things you have forgotten that are worth forgetting. What about that, eh? That is a positive, *sí*?'

He took out a handkerchief and used a folded corner of it to mop up the tears that had trailed down her cheeks. Emelia found it a tender gesture that seemed at odds with his earlier aloofness. Was he finally coming to terms with her inability to remember him?

'What things would I want to forget?' she asked with a puzzled frown.

His eyes shifted away from hers. He refolded the handkerchief and put it in his trouser pocket. 'No marriage is perfect,' he said, 'especially a relatively new one. We had the occasional argument, some of them rather heated at times. Perhaps it is a good thing you can't remember them.'

Emelia tried to read his expression but, apart from a small rueful grimace about his mouth, there was little she could go on. 'What sort of things did we argue about?' she asked.

He gave a one shoulder shrug. 'The usual things. Most of the time little things that got blown all out of proportion.'

She angled her head at him questioningly. 'Who was the first to say sorry?'

There was a slight pause before he answered. 'I am not good at admitting it when I am in the wrong. I guess I take after my father more than I would like in that regard.'

'We all have our pride,' Emelia conceded.

'Yes.' He gave her another brief rueful twist of his mouth. 'Indeed.'

He moved over to a large walk-in wardrobe and opened the sliding doors. 'Your things are in here. You might feel more at home once you are surrounded by your own possessions. The travelling bag you had with you in London was destroyed in the accident.'

Emelia looked at the rows and rows of elegant clothes and shelves of shoes and matching bags. Again, it was like looking into someone else's life. Did *she* wear all these close-fitting designer dresses and sky-high heels? Her eyes went to the other side of the wardrobe where the racks and shelves were empty. She turned and looked at Javier. 'Where are your things?' she asked.

His eyes became shuttered. 'I had Aldana move them into one of the spare rooms for the time being.'

Emelia felt a confusing mixture of relief and disappointment. The relief she could easily explain. The disappointment was a complete mystery to her. 'So—' she quickly ran her tongue over her lips '—so you're not expecting me to...to sleep with you...um...like right away?'

He hooked one dark brow upwards. 'I thought you said you don't usually sleep with perfect strangers?'

She frowned at his tone, not sure if he was teasing her. 'Technically, you're not a stranger, though, are you?' she said. 'I might not remember you, but there's enough evidence around to confirm we are married.'

A glint appeared in his dark-as-night gaze as it held hers. 'Are you inviting me to sleep with you, Emelia?'

Emelia felt her belly fold over itself. 'Er...no...not yet...I mean...no. No. It wouldn't be right for me or even fair to you.'

He came up close, lifting a portion of her hair, slowly twirling it around his finger until she felt the subtle tension on her scalp as he tethered her to him. 'We could do it to see if it unlocks your memory,' he said in a voice that sounded rough and sexy. 'How about it, *querida*? Who knows? Perhaps it is just your mind that has forgotten me. Maybe your body will remember everything.'

Emelia could barely breathe. His chest was brushing against her breasts; she could feel the friction of his shirt through her clothes. Her nipples had sprung to attention, aching and tight, looking for more erotic stimulation. A warm sensation was pooling between her thighs, a pulsing feeling that was part ache, part pleasure, making her want to move forwards to press herself against the hardness she knew instinctively would be there. Her mouth was dry and she sent the point of her tongue out to moisten it, her heart slipping sideways when she saw the way his eyes dropped to follow its passage across her lips.

The pad of his thumb pressed against her bottom lip, setting off livewires of feeling beneath her sensitive skin. 'Such a beautiful mouth,' he said in that low sexy baritone. 'How many times have I kissed it, hmm? How many times has it kissed me?' He pressed himself just that little bit closer, pelvis to pelvis, the swell of his maleness heating her like a hot probe. 'What a pity you can't remember all the delicious things that soft full mouth of yours has done to me in the past.'

Emelia swallowed tightly, the sensation between her thighs turning red hot. She could imagine what she had done; she could see it in his eyes. The erotic pleasure he had experienced with her seemed to be gleaming there to taunt her into recalling every shockingly intimate moment.

His thumb caressed her bottom lip again, pushing against it, watching as it bounced back to fullness as it refilled with blood.

Emelia couldn't take her eyes off his mouth; the enigmatic tilt of it fascinated her. The way he half-smiled, as if he was enjoying the edge he had over her in knowing every sensual pleasure they had shared while she remained in ignorance. Her spine loosened with each stroke of his thumb, the tingling sensation travelling from her lips to every secret place.

'Do you want me to tell you some of the things you did with me, Emelia?' he asked in a gravel-rough tone that made the hairs on the back of her neck lift one by one.

She stood silently staring up at him, like a small nocturnal animal caught in the high beam of headlights: exposed, vulnerable, blinded by feelings she wasn't sure belonged to her. 'I…I'm not sure it would be a good idea to force me to…to remember…' she faltered.

He smiled a lazy smile that made her spine loosen even further. His palm cupped her cheek, holding it gently, each long finger imprinted on her flesh. 'You were shy to begin with, *cariño*,' he said. 'But then perhaps you were shy with your other lovers, *sí*?'

Emelia frowned. 'But I have only had one lover. I must have told you about it, surely? It happened when I was singing in a band in Melbourne. I was too young and didn't realise what I was getting into with someone so much older and experienced. I should have known better, but I was in that rebellious stage a lot of teenagers go through.'

His hand moved from her cheek to rest on her shoulder, his eyes still holding hers like a searchlight. 'You told me some things about it, yes,' he said. 'But then perhaps there are other things you didn't tell me. Things you preferred to keep a secret from me even during our marriage.'

Her frown deepened across her forehead. 'Like what?'

He gave her an inscrutable look and dropped his hand from her shoulder. 'Who knows?' he said. 'You can't remember, or so you say.'

The ensuing silence seemed to ring with the suspicion of his statement.

Emelia sat on the bed in case her legs gave way. 'You think I'm *pretending*?' she asked in an incredulous choked whisper. 'Is that what you think? That I'm making my memory loss up?'

His eyes bored into hers, his mouth pulled tight until his lips were almost flattened. 'You remember nothing of me and yet you grieve like a heartbroken widow over the loss of Marshall.'

She pushed herself upright with her arms. 'Have I not got the right to grieve the loss of a beloved friend?'

His jaw tightened as he held her stare for stare. 'I am your husband, Emelia,' he bit out. 'Your life is with me, not with a dead man.'

She glared back at him furiously. 'You can't force me to stay with you. I might never remember you. What will you do then?'

'Oh, you will remember, Emelia,' he said through clenched teeth, each bitten out word highlighting his accent. 'Make no mistake. You will remember everything.'

Emelia felt a rumble of fear deep and low in her belly. 'I don't know you. I don't even know myself, or at least that's what it feels like it,' she said. 'I don't know who I've become over the past two years. Do you have any idea what it's like for me to step back into the life that was supposedly mine when I don't recognise a thing about it or me?'

He let out a harsh breath. 'Leave it. This is not the time to discuss it.'

'No I can't leave it,' she said. 'You don't seem to trust me. What sort of marriage did we have?'

His eyes were fathomless black pools as they held hers. 'I said I don't wish to discuss this,' he said. 'You need to rest. You are pale and look as if a breath of wind would knock you down.'

'What would you care?' she asked with a churlish look.

'I am not going to continue with this conversation,' he said with an implacable set to his mouth. 'I will leave you to rest. Dinner will be served at eight-thirty. I would suggest you stay close to the villa until you become more familiar with your surroundings. You could easily get lost.'

Emelia sank back down on the mattress once the door had closed on his exit. She put a shaky hand up to her temple, wishing she could unlock the vault of memories that held the secrets of the past two years. What sort of wife was she that her husband didn't seem to trust her? And why did he look at her as if he was torn between pulling her into his arms and showing her the door?

After changing into riding gear, Javier strode down to the stables and, politely declining the offer from his stable-hand, Pedro, quickly saddled his Andalusian stallion, Gitano, and rode out of the villa courtyard. The horse's hooves rattled against the cobblestones but, once the stallion was on the grass of the fields leading to the woods, Javier let him have his head. The feel of the powerful muscles of his horse beneath him was just the shot of adrenalin he needed to distract himself from being with Emelia again.

Holding her in his arms when she had cried had been like torture. He couldn't remember a time when she had shown such emotion before. She was usually so cool and in control of herself. It had stirred things in him to fever pitch to have her so close. Her body had felt so warm and soft against his, so achingly familiar. He could so easily have pushed her down on the bed and reclaimed her as his. His body had throbbed to possess her. It disgusted him that he was so weak. Had he learned nothing? Women were not to be trusted, especially women like his runaway wife.

He had noted every nuance of her face on the journey home to Spain. If she truly had forgotten how wealthy he was, she was in no doubt of it now. Even if she did recall what a sham their marriage had become, she was unlikely to admit it now. Why would she? He could give her everything money could buy. Her lover was dead. She had no one else to turn to, nowhere else to go. She was back in his life due to a quirk of fate. There was no way now that he could toss her out as he had sworn he would do when he'd found out about her affair. The public would not look upon him kindly for divorcing his amnesiac wife. But there could be benefits in keeping her close to his side, he conceded. He still wanted her. That much had not changed, even though it annoyed him that he could not dismiss his attraction for her as easily as he wanted to. It had been there right from the beginning; the electric pulse of wanting that fizzled between them whenever they were within touching distance. She might not recognise him mentally but he felt sure her body was responding to him the way it always had. It would not take him long to have her writhing and twisting beneath him; all memory of her lover would be replaced with new memories of him and him alone.

He would cut her from his life when he was sure she was back on her feet. Their marriage would have fulfilled its purpose by then, in any case. Their divorce would be swift and final. All contact with her would cease from that point. He had no intention of keeping her with him indefinitely, not after the scandal she had caused him. The public would forget in time as new scandals were uncovered, but he could not.

He *would* not.

The horse's hooves thundered over the fields, the wind rushing through Javier's hair as he rode at breakneck speed. He pulled the stallion to a halt at the top of the hill, surveying the expanse of his estate below. The grey-green of the olive groves and the fertile fields of citrus and almonds reminded him of all he had worked so hard and long for. For all the sacrifices he had made to keep this property within his hands. His father's gambling and risky business deals had cost Javier dearly. He'd had to compromise himself in ways he had never dreamed possible. But what was done was done and it could not be undone. It eased his conscience only slightly that he hadn't done it for himself. Izabella had a right to her inheritance, and he had made sure it was not going to be whittled away by his father's home-wrecking widow.

The stallion tossed his head and snorted, his hooves drumming in the dust with impatience. Javier stroked the stallion's silky powerful neck, speaking low and soothingly in Spanish. The horse rose on his hindquarters, his front hooves pawing at the air. Javier laughed as he thought of his wayward wife and how fate had handed her back to him to do with her as he wished. He turned the horse and galloped him back down through the forest to the plains below, the thrill of the ride nothing to what waited for him at the end of it.

Emelia ignored the comfort of the big bed and, after a refreshing shower and change of clothes, went on a solitary tour of the villa in the hope of triggering something in her brain. Most of the rooms were too formal for her taste. They were almost austere, with their priceless works of art and uncomfortable-looking antiquated furniture. She couldn't help wondering why she hadn't gone about redecorating the place. Money was certainly no object, but perhaps she'd felt intimidated by the age and history of the villa. It was certainly very old. Every wall of the place seemed to have a portrait of an ancestor on it, each pair of eyes following her in what she felt to be an accusatory silence. She found it hard to imagine a small child feeling at home here. Was this the place where Javier had grown up? There was so much she didn't know about him, or at least no longer knew.

She breathed out a sigh as she opened yet another door. This one led into a library-cum-study. Three walls of floor to ceiling bookshelves and a leather-topped desk dominated the space, but she could see a collection of photo frames beside the laptop computer on the desk, which drew her like a magnet. The floorboards creaked beneath the old rugs as she walked to the desk, the hairs on the back of her neck lifting like antennae.

'Don't be stupid,' she scolded herself. 'There's no such thing as ghosts.' But, even so, when she looked at the photographs she felt as if she were encountering something supernatural—the ghost of who she had been for the past two years.

She picked up the first frame and studied it for a

moment. It was a photo of her lying on a blanket in an olive grove, the sun coming down at an angle, highlighting her honey-blonde hair and grey-blue eyes. She was smiling coquettishly at the camera, flirting with whoever was behind the camera lens.

She put the frame down and picked up the next one, her heart giving a little skip when she saw Javier with his arms wrapped around her from behind, his tall frame slightly stooped as his chin rested on the top of her head, his smile wide and proud as he faced the camera. She could almost feel his hard body pressing into her back, the swell of his arousal, the pulse and thrum of his blood…

The door of the study suddenly opened and Emelia dropped the frame, the glass shattering on the floor at her feet. She stood frozen for a moment as Javier stepped into the room, closing the door with a click that sounded like a prison cell being locked.

'Don't touch it,' he commanded when she began to bend at the knees. 'You might cut yourself.'

'I'm sorry…' Emelia said, glancing down at the floor before meeting his gaze. 'You frightened me.'

His black eyes didn't waver as they held hers. 'I can assure you that was not my intention.'

Emelia swallowed as he approached the desk. He was wearing a white casual polo shirt and beige jodhpurs and long black leather riding boots, looking every inch the brooding hero of a Regency novel. He smelt of the outdoors with a hint of horse and hay and something that was essentially male, essentially *him*. He filled her nostrils with it, making her feel as if she was being cast under an intoxicating spell. His tall authoritarian presence, that aura of command he wore like an extra layer of skin, that air of arrogance and assuredness that was so at odds with her insecurities and doubts and memory blanks. 'I…I was trying to see if anything in here jogged my memory,' she tried her best to explain.

He hooked a brow upwards. 'And did it?'

She bit her lower lip, glancing at the shattered glass on the floor, which seemed to sever them as a couple. Was it symbolic in some way? A shard of glass was lying across their smiling faces, almost cutting them in two. She brought her gaze back to his. 'No…' She let out a sigh. 'I don't remember when that photo was taken or where.'

He bent down and carefully removed the remaining pieces of glass from the photo frame before placing it back on the desk. 'It was taken a few days after we got home from our honeymoon. I took you for a picnic to one of the olive groves on the estate. The other photo with us together was taken in Rome.'

Emelia ran her tongue over her dry lips before asking, 'Where did we go for our honeymoon?'

He was standing close, too close. She felt the alarm bells of her senses start to ring when he stepped even closer. The wall of bookshelves was at her back, each ancient tome threatening to come down and smother her. His dark eyes meshed with hers, holding them entranced. She felt her heart give a knock against her breastbone in anticipation of that sensuous mouth coming down to hers. She suddenly realised how much she wanted that mouth to soften against hers, to kiss her tenderly, lingeringly, to explore every corner of her mouth in intimate detail.

He placed his hand under the curtain of her hair, his

fingers warm and dry against the sensitive skin of her neck. 'Where do you think we went?' he asked.

Emelia's teeth sank into her bottom lip, her brain working overtime. 'Um…Paris?'

His hand stilled and one of his dark brows lifted. 'Was that a guess or do you remember something?' he asked.

'I've always dreamed of honeymooning in Paris,' she said. 'It's supposed to be the most romantic city in the world. And I saw the stamp on my passport so I suppose it wasn't such a wild guess.'

He continued to hold her gaze for endless moments, his fingers moving in a rhythmic motion at her nape. 'Your dream came true, Emelia,' he said. 'I gave you a honeymoon to surpass all honeymoons.'

She sucked half of her bottom lip into her mouth, releasing it to say, 'I'm sorry. You must be thinking what a shocking waste of money it was now that I can't even recall a second of it.'

He gave a couldn't-care-less shrug. 'We can have a second honeymoon, *sí*? One that you will never forget.'

Emelia's eyes went to his mouth of their own volition. He was smiling that sexy half-smile again, the one that made her blood race through her veins. What was it about this man that made her so breathless with excitement? It was as if he only had to look at her and she was a trembling mass of needs and wants. She felt the tingling of her skin as he touched her with those long fingers. The fingers that had clearly touched her in places she wasn't sure she wanted to think about. He knew her so well and yet he was still a stranger to her.

A second honeymoon?

Her belly turned over itself. How could she sleep

with a man she didn't know? It would be nothing but physical attraction, an animal instinct, an impulse she had never felt compelled to respond to before.

Or had she?

How did she know what their history was? She could only go on what he had told her. She hadn't thought herself the type to fall in love so rapidly, to marry someone within weeks of meeting them. But then maybe she hadn't fallen in love with him. Maybe she had fallen in lust. She shied away from the thought but it kept creeping back to taunt her. He was so dangerously attractive. She could feel the pull of his magnetism even now, the thrill of him touching her, the stroke of his fingers so drugging she could feel herself capitulating second by second. His eyes were dark pools of mystery, luring her in, making her drown in their enigmatic depths. She felt her eyelids come down to half mast, her breathing becoming choppy as his hand stilled at the back of her neck, pressing her forwards with a gentle but determined action as his mouth came within a breath of hers.

'D-don't…' Her voice came out hoarse, uncertain and not at all convincing.

His hand still cupped the nape of her neck, warm and strong, supportive and yet determined. 'Don't what?' he asked in a low deep burr.

She swallowed. 'You know what…'

'Is it not right for a husband to kiss his wife?' he asked.

'But I…I don't feel like your wife,' Emelia said breathlessly.

There was a three beat pause as his dark eyes locked on hers.

'Then it is about time you did,' he said and, swooping down, covered her mouth with his.

CHAPTER FOUR

EMELIA'S heart almost stopped when his mouth touched down on hers. The raw male scent of him was intoxicating, dangerous, and that alone would have had her senses spinning, but the pressure of his lips upon hers drew from her a response she wasn't entirely sure she should be giving. He cradled her head in his hands, giving her no room to pull away even if she had the wherewithal to do so. The contact of his mouth on hers was explorative at first, light, tentative almost, but then, with just one very masculine stroke of his tongue, everything changed.

Her lips opened to him as if of their own volition, instinctively, welcoming him inside the moist cave of her mouth. Her tongue met his briefly, flirting around it, dancing with it until finally mating with it at its command. He subdued her with the power of each stroke and thrust of his tongue, teasing her into submission, relishing the victory by crushing his mouth to hers with increasing pressure. Emelia felt the surge of his body against her, his arousal so thick and hard it made her realise how much history existed between them, a history she had yet to discover. Her body, however, seemed familiar with it. It was reacting with fervour to every movement of his mouth on hers, her arms automatically going around his neck, holding him to her as if she had done it many times before, her pelvis seeking the hardened throb of his, her inner core melting with longing. Her breasts bloomed with pleasure against the contact with his hard chest, her nipples tightening to buds, aching to feel the slippery warmth of his mouth and tongue.

His mouth moved from hers on a searing pathway down the side of her neck, slowly, sensuously bringing every nerve to gasping, startled life. Goosebumps rose all over her skin as he discovered the delicate scaffold of her collarbone, his tongue dipping into the tiny dish of her tender flesh. His lips feathered against her skin as he spoke in a low sexy tone. 'You taste of vanilla.'

Emelia felt electric jolts shoot up and down her legs at the thought of where that mouth and tongue had been on her body. She could almost feel its pathway now, the way her secret feminine flesh was pulsing, as if in anticipation of him claiming it. She clutched at his head with her fingers, feeling the thick strands of his dark hair move like silk beneath her fingertips.

'I want you.' He mouthed the words against her neck, making her nerves leap and dance again. 'God, but I want you.'

'W-we can't...' Emelia gasped as his mouth showered kisses all over her face: over her eyelids, over her cheeks, her nose and so temptingly close to her tingling, swollen lips.

'What's to stop us?' he said in a husky tone as he pressed a hot moist kiss to her trembling mouth. 'We are married, are we not?'

Emelia was too drunk on his kiss to answer. His tongue went in search of hers again, mating with it in an erotic tango that left her gasping with need. His kiss was hungry, demanding, leaving her in no doubt of where it was leading. It was a pre-sex kiss, blatant in its intent, shockingly intimate as his hands moved from cradling her head, sliding down her bare arms to encircle her wrists. The latent strength of him sent a shiver of reaction through her. He was so strong; she was so weak, but not just in physical strength. Her will-power seemed to have totally evaporated. She was molten wax in his arms, fitting to his hard form as if she had known no other place.

He released her hands and moved his up under her top, sliding his warm palms over her belly and her ribcage. Her heart gave a lurching movement as his fingers splayed over her possessively. Emelia thought she would die if he didn't touch her breasts and she moved against him, silently pleading for him to pleasure her.

His hand cupped her and she let out a tiny whimper of pleasure, for even through the fine lace of her bra she could feel the tantalising heat of his touch. 'You want more, *querida*?' he asked softly, seductively.

Emelia gasped as he pushed aside the cobweb of lace, his fingers skating over her burgeoning flesh. His thumb lingered over her engorged nipple, moving back and forth, hot little rubs that lifted every hair on her scalp.

'You want this, *sí*?' he said and bent his mouth to her breast and suckled softly at first and then harder.

Emelia's fingers clutched at his hair, trying to anchor herself as delicious sensations washed through her. 'Oh… Oh, God…' she whimpered.

'You like this too,' he said and swept his tongue down the outer curve of her breast, licking like a jungle cat, the sexy rasp of his tongue melting every vertebrae of her spine into trembling submission.

'And this,' he added, pressing her back against the desk, his thighs parting hers with shockingly primal intention.

Emelia's passion-glazed eyes flew open and her hands thrust against his chest. 'N-no…' she said but it came out so hoarsely she had to repeat it. 'No…no, I can't.'

One of his dark brows hooked upwards, his body still poised against hers. 'No?'

She shook her head, her teeth sinking into her lower lip as her eyes momentarily fell away from his.

He let out a theatrical sigh and straightened, pulling her upright against him, his hands settling on her waist, his powerful body, hot, aroused and hard, just a breath's distance away. 'That wasn't what you used to say,' he said with a taunting gleam in his dark eyes. 'This was one of your favourite places for a quick—'

Emelia pushed two of her fingertips against his mouth, blocking off the coarse word she was almost certain he intended to use. 'Please…don't…' she said hollowly.

He peeled her fingers away from his mouth, kissing the tips one by one, his bottomless eyes holding hers. 'Don't you want to be reminded of how sensually adventurous you were, Emelia?' he asked.

Her throat rose and fell over a tight swallow. 'No… no, I don't.'

He pressed a soft kiss to the middle of her palm and then dipped his tongue right into the middle of it, hotly, moistly, his eyes still locked with hers. 'I taught you everything you know,' he went on. 'You were so eager to learn. A straight A student, in fact.'

She closed her eyes tight. 'Stop it. Stop doing this.'

'Open your eyes, Emelia,' he commanded.

She scrunched them even tighter. 'No.'

His hands went to her waist, holding her against his rock-hard arousal. 'This is what you do to me, *querida*,' he said in a sexy growl.

Emelia wrenched out of his hold with a strength she had no conscious knowledge of possessing. Her chest heaved with the effort as she stood, trembling and shaken, a few feet away. She folded her arms across her chest, fighting for breath, fighting for control, fighting for some self-respect, which seemed to have gone AWOL some minutes ago.

Javier gave her an indolent smile. 'What are you frightened of, *mi amor*?' he asked.

'I don't know you,' Emelia said.

'But you want me, all the same.'

'I'm not myself right now.' She tightened her arms beneath her breasts. 'I don't know what I want.'

'Your body remembers me, Emelia. It wants me. You can't deny it.'

Emelia moved even further away because she had a sneaking suspicion what he said was true. Every sense was alive to him, to his presence and to his touch. She could still taste him in her mouth, the musky male heat of him lingering there like a fine wine on her palate. Was he an addiction she had developed over the last two years? How could any woman resist such incredible potency? He oozed sensual heat through the pores of his skin. She felt the waves of attraction tighten the air she breathed in. Every part of her body he had touched was still tingling with the need for more. His incendiary suggestion was still ringing in her ears, making her mind race with erotic scenarios: of her spread before him like a feast; her legs open to his powerful thrusting body, her senses in a vortex of sensation, her back arching in pleasure, her mouth falling open in sharp, high cries of ecstasy.

He came to where she was standing, her back pressed against the bookshelves, his eyes smouldering so darkly they seemed to strip her bare. 'Maybe it was a mistake for me to move out of our room,' he said. 'Perhaps I should insist on you sleeping with me, even though you can't remember me.'

Emelia's back felt as if it was being bitten into by the shelves. 'You c-can't mean that,' she said croakily.

He tipped up her chin, holding her frightened gaze with the powerful beam of his. 'Making love with me might trigger something in your brain. It might be the part of the missing puzzle, *sí*?'

His disturbing presence was triggering all sorts of things in her body, let alone her brain, Emelia thought in rising panic. She placed her hands on his chest with the intention of pushing him away again, but the feel of his hard muscles under her palms sent off a little flashbulb in her head. It was a tiny spark of memory, a pinpoint of light in the darkness. She splayed her fingers experimentally and, as if of their own accord, her fingertips began moving over his hard flat nipples, over his perfectly sculptured pectoral muscles and up to his neck, where she could see a pulse beating like a hammer beneath his skin. She moved her fingertips to the raspy skin of his lean jaw, the prickle of his stubble sending tantalising little tingles right up her arms.

'What is it?' he asked, holding her hand against his face with the broad span of his. 'Have you remembered something?'

She frowned as she fought to retrieve the fleeting image. It was like the shadow of a ghost, barely visible, but she could sense its presence. 'I don't know…' She bit down on her lip, pulling her hand out from under his. 'I thought for a minute…but I just don't know…'

He picked up her hand again and held it against his mouth, his lips feathering against her curled up fingers as he spoke. 'Touch me again, *cariño*,' he commanded softly. 'Touch is an important part of memory. Taste and smell, too.'

Emelia uncurled her fingers and carefully traced the outline of his lips, her fingertip grazing against his stubble again. She felt transfixed by the shape of his mouth, the way his top lip was carved almost harshly and yet his lower one was so generous and sensual. He drew her fingertip into his mouth and sucked on it. It was such an intimate thing to do, flagrantly sexual, especially when his eyes captured hers and glinted at her meaningfully. She pulled out of his hold once more, gathering herself with an effort. 'I'm sorry,' she said crisply. 'I don't remember anything.'

His expression gave little away but Emelia sensed a thread of anger stringing his words together as he spoke. 'I will leave you to rest before dinner. Leave this.' He indicated the broken glass on the floor. 'I will get Aldana to clean it up later. If you need anything just press nine on the telephone by the bed upstairs. It is a direct line to Aldana's quarters. She will bring you some tea or coffee or a cool drink if you should require it.'

She watched as he strode out of the library, the squeak of the expensive leather of his riding boots the only sound in the silence.

Emelia woke from a nap feeling totally disoriented, her heart beating like the wings of a frightened bird as she sat upright on the big bed. She put a hand to her throat, trying to control her breathing to bring down her panic to a manageable level. She dragged herself off the bed and stumbled into the en suite bathroom. Seeing her reflection was like looking at another version of herself, a more sophisticated and yet unhappier version. She put a fingertip to each of her sharp cheekbones. Her mouth was pulled down at the corners as if smiling had become a chore. Her eyes looked tired but also a little haunted, as if they were keeping secrets they didn't really want to keep.

She washed her face with cold water and then turned and looked longingly at the huge spa bath next to the double shower cubicle. She had at least an hour before dinner and the thought of sinking into a huge bath tub full of fragrant bubbles was too much for her to resist.

The water lapped at her aching limbs as she lowered herself into the bath, the scent of honeysuckle filling the air, reminding her of the hot summers and long lazy days of her childhood back in Australia. She closed her eyes and laid her head back, her body relaxing for the first time since she had woken from the coma.

Even in her languid repose, it was hard not to think of Peter. The thought of him lying in a cold dark grave was surreal when it seemed only a few days ago they were having coffee together at the end of her session at The Silver Room. The police had told her it had been a high speed accident but the knowledge hadn't sat well with her. Peter had lost a close mate in a car accident when he was a teenager. His intractable stance on reckless and dangerous driving was one of the things she had admired about him—one of the many things. During their youth, he had hinted more than once that he wanted more than a platonic friendship from her but she had let him down as gently as she could. While they had been close friends and had many interests in common, she had never envisaged him as an intimate partner. She had always looked on him as a brother. There was no chemistry, or at least not from her point of view. She knew it was different for men, and Peter had not been an exception. She had seen his head turned by many beautiful women who came into his hotel bar. She knew men's desires were more often than not fuelled by their vision. Sex was a physical drive that could just as easily be performed with a perfect stranger.

Emelia felt her belly give a distinct wobble when she thought of the stranger who was her husband. She saw raw unbridled desire in Javier's eyes; it smouldered there like hot coals every time he looked at her. He had openly declared how much he wanted her. She had heard the erotic promise in the words. It was not a matter of *if* but *when*.

He knew it.

She knew it.

Emelia looked down at her breasts, her rosy nipples just peeping out of the water amidst the bubbles, a riot of sensations rippling through her as she thought of how he had caressed her earlier. He had touched her with such possessive familiarity. Was that why she had responded so instinctively? She felt her insides give another fluttery movement as she thought about him possessing her totally. Would she remember him in the throes of making love as he suggested? She reared back from her thoughts like a horse shying at a jump. It was too soon to be taking that step. She couldn't possibly give herself to a man she didn't know.

But you're married to him, a little voice reminded her.

And you're attracted to him, another voice piped up.

Emelia slipped under the water to escape her traitorous thoughts, holding her breath for as long as she dared...

Javier tapped on the bathroom door but there was no answer. It was quiet. Too quiet. There was not even the sound of running or splashing water.

He opened the door and when he saw Emelia's slim body lying submerged in the bath he felt a hand clutch at his insides.

'Emelia!' He rushed to the tub and grabbed her under the armpits, hauling her upright as water splashed everywhere.

She gave a gasping cry of shock, her wet hair like seaweed all over her face. 'What do you think you're doing?' she spluttered.

Javier waited until his heart had returned to his chest from where it had leapt into his throat. 'I thought you were unconscious,' he explained in a voice that sounded as ragged as he felt. 'I thought you might have hit your head again or something.'

She flashed him a livid glare as she hastily crossed

her arms over her breasts. 'You could have knocked before you came barging in.'

'I did knock.' He stepped out of the puddle of water he was standing in, glancing ruefully at his sodden trousers and shoes. 'You didn't answer.'

Her knees bent upwards, shielding her chest even further. 'You had no right to come in without my permission,' she said.

He sent one of his brows up in a mocking slant. 'That little knock on the head has turned you into a prude, eh, Emelia? I remember a time not so long ago when you made room for me in there.' He bent down and scooped up a handful of bubbles, holding them just above her bent knees. 'Do you want to know what we got up to?'

She stiffened as if the water had turned to ice around her. 'Get out,' she said in a clipped voice.

Javier let the bubbles fall from his hand, his eyes unwavering on hers. He felt her tension, the way she gave a tiny, almost imperceptible flinch as each cluster of bubbles slid down from her kneecaps and down her thighs to slowly dissipate as they landed on the surface of the water. As each throbbing second passed he could hear the soft popping sound of the lather gradually losing its vigour. Within minutes the soapy shield she was hiding behind would be gone.

In spite of her betrayal, he felt his body surge with excitement. Hot rushing blood filled his groin, the ache for release so quick, so urgent it made him realise how hard it was going to be to keep his distance from her. But then wanting her had always been his problem, his one true vulnerability.

From that first moment he had heard her clever little fingers playing those lilting cadences when he'd walked into The Silver Room, he had felt something deep inside shift into place. She had looked up from the piano, her fingers stumbling over a note as their eyes had locked. He had smiled at her with his eyes—that was all it had taken—and she had been his.

He looked down at her now, wondering if she had any idea of the war going on inside him. She was cautious around him, understandable given she no longer recognised him, but he felt the sexual undertow of her gaze every time it meshed with his. It would not take him long to have her back in his bed and threshing in his arms as she used to do. But would that finally dissolve the anger and hatred he felt whenever he thought of her with the man she had run away to be with?

'It is not the behaviour of a devoted wife to order her husband out of his own bathroom,' Javier said, breaking the taut silence.

'I…I don't care,' she said, her teeth chattering slightly.

He plucked a bath sheet off the warming rail and held it just out of her reach. 'You'd better get out. You're starting to get cold.'

Her grey-blue eyes battled with his. 'I'm not getting out until you leave.'

He settled his tall frame into a trenchant stance. 'I am not leaving until you get out.'

She clenched her teeth, her voice coming out as a hiss, reminding him of a snarling cat. 'Why are you doing this? Why are you being such a beast?'

'What is all the fuss about, *querida*?' he asked evenly. 'I have seen you naked countless times.'

Her throat rose and fell. 'It's different now… You know that…'

He came closer with the towel, unfolding it for her to step into. 'Come on, Emelia. You are shivering.'

She flattened her mouth and, giving him another livid glare, stood and grasped for the towel, covering herself haphazardly, but not before he feasted his eyes on her slim feminine form. There were catwalk models who had less going for them, Javier thought. With her coltish long legs and beautifully toned arms and those small high breasts with their delectable rosy nipples, it was all he could do not to pull her out of the slippery tub and crush his body to hers. How many times had he tasted the sweet honey of her feminine body? How many times had he plunged into her, his cataclysmic release unlike any he had ever experienced with anyone else? As much as it felt like a dagger in his gut, he wondered how it had been with her lover. Had she gone down on him with the same fervour? Had she whispered words of love to him in the afterglow of lovemaking? Javier felt his top lip curl as he watched her try to cover herself more effectively. 'You are wasting your time, Emelia,' he said. 'I know every inch of your body and you know every inch of mine.'

Her eyes shifted away from his, her throat doing that nervous up and down thing again. 'I would like some privacy,' she said, wiping her brow with the back of her hand. 'I…I'm not feeling well.'

Javier's brows shot together. 'Why didn't you tell me?' he asked. 'What is wrong? A headache? The doctor said headaches are common after—'

'It's not a bad one, just an ache behind one eye.' She brushed at her damp brow once more, this time with a corner of the towel. 'It's making me feel a little nauseous. Perhaps it's the change of climate. It's a lot hotter here than in England.'

'You were only in London a week,' he pointed out. 'Hardly time to be reacclimatising, don't you think?'

Her gaze returned to his, two small frown lines sectioning her forehead. 'Oh…yes…yes, of course…I forgot.' She pressed her lips together and looked away.

Javier saw the shadow of grief pass through her eyes before she averted her gaze. He fought down his anger, reminding himself she was with him now. His rival was dead. It was just Emelia and him now, to get on with their lives as best they could. 'Dinner is not long away,' he said. 'I will need to get changed. Do you want me to escort you downstairs or do you think you will find your way?'

She clutched at the towel as she looked at him with her guarded gaze. 'I'll find my own way…thank you.'

He gave a brisk nod and left the bathroom.

Emelia opened the wardrobe and, searching through the array of clothes, selected a simple black dress and heels to match. As she dressed she couldn't quite suppress the feeling that she was dressing in someone else's clothes. The dress was made by a French designer and must have cost a fortune; the shoes, too, were a brand celebrities and Hollywood stars regularly wore. She used the cosmetics in the drawer in the en suite bathroom, but only lightly and, after drying her hair with a blow-dryer, she left it lying about her shoulders.

As she came down the grand staircase she heard Javier's voice from the study. He was speaking in Spanish and sounded angry. Emelia knew it was probably beneath her to eavesdrop but, even so, she couldn't resist pausing outside the closed study door. Of course hearing only one side of a conversation was not all that revealing and, although she understood very basic Spanish, he spoke so rapidly she found it hard to follow everything he said. One or two sentences did stand out, however.

'There is not going to be a divorce.'

Emelia's eyes widened as she listened even harder, wincing as one or two expletives were uttered before his next statement.

'The money is not yours and never has been and, as long as I live, it never will be.'

The phone slammed down and, before Emelia could move even a couple of paces down the hall, Javier came storming out of the study. He pulled up short as if someone had jerked him back by the back of his jacket when he saw her standing there with guilt written all over her face.

'How long have you been standing out here?' He almost barked the words at her.

Emelia took a layer of her lip gloss off with the nervous dart of her tongue. 'I…I was just walking past. I heard you raise your voice.'

His expression was thunderous but Emelia had a feeling the anger was not directed at her. He raked a hand through his hair and released a heavy sigh, as if deliberately trying to suppress his fury. 'Just as well you don't remember any Spanish,' he said. 'I don't usually swear in the presence of women, but my father's third wife is nothing but a gold-digging, trouble-making tramp.'

Emelia wondered if she should tell him she could speak and understand a little of his language, but in that nanosecond of hesitation she decided against it. Wouldn't it seem strange that she couldn't remember him and yet she could remember every word of Spanish she had learned over the past two years? After all, he had already implied she might be pretending. Why he would think that was beyond her, although, given the conversation she had just overheard, it made her wonder if their marriage had been as happy as he had intimated. She had just heard him say there was not going to be a divorce. Did that mean there had been recent speculation about their marriage ending? Javier had mentioned how the press had made some scurrilous comments about her relationship with Peter Marshall. There would be few men who would cope well with their private life being splashed all over the papers and gossip magazines, but Javier struck her as a particularly proud and intensely private man. There was so much she didn't know and she didn't feel comfortable asking in case the answers he gave were not the ones she wanted to hear.

'It must be very difficult for you, under the circumstances,' she offered.

He gave her a long look and sighed again, taking her elbow to lead the way to the dining room. 'My father was a fool leaving Izabella's mother for Claudine Marsden. That woman is a home wrecker. Why he couldn't see it is beyond me.'

'Some men are like that,' she said. 'My father is the same.'

He glanced down at her as they came to the dining room door. 'Did your father contact you while you were in hospital?' he asked.

Emelia's mouth tightened. 'No, why should he? As far as he is concerned, I am as good as dead to him. He told me he never wanted to see me again. I have no reason to suspect he didn't mean it.'

Javier pressed his lips together, a frown creasing his

forehead as he led her to the table. 'People say all sorts of things in the heat of the moment.' He paused before adding, 'I should have phoned him. I didn't think of it, I'm afraid. There was so much going on at the time. He should have been notified about the accident.'

'Did I at some point give you his contact details?' Emelia asked.

'No, but it wouldn't have been all that hard to track him down,' he said. 'Would you like me to make contact now, just to let him know you are all right?'

Emelia thought about her father with his new wife, who was only three years older than her. After their last insult-throwing argument, she couldn't see him flying all the way to Spain with flowers and a get well card in hand. He was probably sunning himself at his luxurious Sunshine Coast mansion with his child bride waiting on him hand and foot. 'No, don't bother,' she said, trying to remove the bitterness from her tone. 'He's probably got much more important things to see to.'

Javier gave her a thoughtful look as he drew out her chair.

Emelia took the seat, waiting until he sat down opposite to say, 'Our backgrounds—apart from the level of wealth—are very similar, aren't they? Your father was estranged from you and mine from me. Is that something that drew us together when we first met?'

His dark eyes held hers for a moment before he answered. 'It was one of many things.'

'What were some of the other things?' she asked.

He poured wine for each of them, his mouth tilting slightly. 'Lust, lust and more lust,' he said.

Emelia pursed her lips, hating that she was blushing,

hating him for watching with such mocking amusement. 'I can assure you I would never fall in lust with someone,' she said. 'I would only ever love someone I admired as a man, for his qualities as a person, not his possessions or social standing. And I most certainly wouldn't marry a man on physical attraction alone.'

His mocking smile was still in place. 'So you must have loved me, eh, Emelia?' He flicked his napkin across his lap, his eyes still tethering hers. 'The thing is, will you remember to love me again?'

CHAPTER FIVE

EMELIA placed her own napkin over her lap, all the time avoiding those black-as-pitch eyes. The hairs on the back of her neck were tingling and her stomach was rolling like a ball going down a very steep hill. Had she felt like this during their marriage? Had her skin felt prickly and sensitive just with his gaze on her, let alone his touch? She desperately wanted to remember everything about him, everything about them—their relationship, the love they supposedly had shared.

Or had they?

The thought slipped into her mind, unfurling like a curl of smoke beneath a closed door. Did he love her the way she had evidently loved him? It was so difficult to know what he felt; he kept himself to himself most of the time. She understood his reluctance to reveal his feelings, given her loss of memory. He might resent looking a fool if she never regained her memory of him. In any case, the doctors had warned him not to pressure her. Was that why he was acting like the perfect stranger, polite but aloof, with just occasional glimpses of his personality? There was so much she didn't know about him, things she would need to know in order to navigate her way through the complex labyrinth her mind had become. With an effort she raised her eyes back to his. 'I feel such a fool for not asking you this earlier, but what is it you do for a living?'

'I buy and sell businesses,' he said. 'I own and head an international company. We do work all over the world. That was why I have been in Moscow a lot lately. I have a big deal I am working on. It requires a lot of intense negotiation.'

Emelia sat quietly absorbing that information, hoping it would trigger something in her brain. She looked at his hands as they poured wine into both of their glasses. She could imagine him being a formidable opponent in business, his quick mind and sharp intelligence setting him apart from his rivals. 'What sort of businesses do you buy?' she asked.

'Ailing ones,' he said. 'I buy them and reinvent them and sell them for a profit.' He hitched one shoulder indifferently. 'It's a living.'

Emelia picked up her crystal wine glass. 'Apparently quite a good one.' She took a tentative sip and put the glass back down. 'Was your father in the same field of work?'

'No, he was in retail,' he said. 'Electrical, mostly. He had several outlets in Spain. He expected me to go into the business with him but I never wanted that for myself. Selling refrigerators and televisions and toasters never appealed to me. I wanted more of a challenge.'

'Is that what caused the rift between you?'

'That and other things,' he said, frowning slightly as he returned his glass to the table.

Aldana came in with their starters and, while she was serving them, Emelia thought about Javier's background. There was no shortage of wealth; the private jet, the villa and grounds and the staff to maintain it must cost a fortune. Had he inherited it from his father or accumulated it himself? He must be very good at what he did. No one could buy a company without a huge amount of money behind them. And if he was buying and selling more than one and all over the world, he must be far more successful than she had thought. She decided to check out his profile on the Internet later, to see a little more into the man she was married to.

'*Gracias*, Aldana,' Javier said as the housekeeper left with a sour look in Emelia's direction, which she was sure he didn't see. Emelia wondered if she should comment on it but then decided against it. Maybe Javier would think she was making trouble. Aldana seemed very much a part of the woodwork of the villa. But it worried Emelia that the housekeeper had not warmed to her over the last two years. She was not used to people disliking her on sight. It made her feel as if she didn't know herself any more. Who was she now? Why had the housekeeper taken such an active dislike to her?

A moment or two of silence passed.

'Is the wine not to your liking?' Javier asked. 'It used to be one of your favourites.'

Emelia wrinkled her nose. 'Sorry, I guess my palate has changed or something. I'll stick to water. I need the fluids, in any case.'

'Would you like me to call a doctor?' he asked. 'You might have picked up a bug in the hospital.'

'No, I'm fine.' She twisted her mouth wryly. 'To tell you the truth, I'm a little sick of doctors. I just want to get well again.'

He gave her a tight smile. 'Of course.'

Emelia picked at her main course after Aldana had brought it in, but with little appetite. The tight band of tension around her forehead she had been trying so hard to ignore was making her feel ill again. All she could think of was retreating to the sanctuary of bed.

'You're really not feeling well, are you?' Javier asked once the housekeeper had cleared the plates.

Emelia gave him an apologetic grimace. 'I'm sorry. My headache's been getting worse all evening.'

He rose from the table and gently helped her out of her chair. 'Come on,' he said. 'I'll take you upstairs and help you get settled. Are you sure about the doctor? What if I just make a call to ask his opinion?'

'No, please don't bother. Dr Pratchett told me head-aches are common sometimes up to weeks after a head injury. I just need a painkiller and sleep.'

Javier left the bedroom while Emelia changed into nightwear and after a few minutes he came back in with a glass of water and a couple of painkillers. Once she had taken them, he took the glass and set it down on the bedside table. 'I have to fly back to Moscow tomorrow,' he said, sitting on the edge of the bed next to her. 'I just got a phone call while I was downstairs. I am sorry about the short notice but, with the accident and every-thing, I had to cut short my business there.'

'I'm sorry to have been such a bother—'

He placed a hand over hers, silencing her. 'I have given Aldana and the others instructions to keep a watch over you. I will only be away two days, three at the most.'

'I'm perfectly able to look after myself.' She pulled her hand out from under his and crossed her arms over her chest. 'I don't need to be watched over like a small child.'

'Emelia, there are journalists lurking about looking for a story,' he said. 'If you set foot outside the villa grounds you will be under siege. You are not well enough to fend off their intrusive questions. You will end up even more confused and disoriented.'

Her grey-blue eyes narrowed slightly. 'Are these precautions for me or for you?'

He squared his shoulders. 'What exactly are you implying?'

She bit down on her bottom lip so hard it went white. 'I don't know what's going on,' she said. 'I don't know what's what any more. You say we were happily married, but you don't seem to like me, let alone love me.'

Javier placed his hand on the curve of her cheek, turning her head to face him. 'This is not the time to be talking about my feelings,' he said. 'This is the time for you to concentrate on getting well again. That's why I want you to stay within the confines of the villa grounds.'

'What did I used to do to occupy myself when you went away on business?' she asked.

Javier would have dearly liked to ask her the same thing. How long had her affair gone on, for instance? How many times had she met her lover while he was abroad on business? How many of her 'shopping trips' to London been a cover for other activities? 'You used the gym in the building near the pool and you occasionally practised the piano.'

She frowned as she looked down at her manicured hands with their elegant French-polished nails. When had she stopped biting her nails? And how on earth did she play the piano with them so long? She looked up at him after a moment. 'So I wasn't teaching?'

'No. You said you were no longer interested in teaching children,' he said. 'You said it didn't suit your lifestyle any more.'

She was still frowning. '*I* said that?'

Javier studied her for a moment. 'You said a lot of things, Emelia.'

'What other things did I say?' she asked.

'You didn't want children, for one thing,' he said. 'You were adamant about it.'

Her eyes widened. 'Not want children?'

He nodded. 'You didn't want to be tied down.'

She put a hand to her head, as if to check it was still there. 'I can't believe I didn't want kids. That seems so…so selfish.' She looked at him again. 'Did *you* want children?'

'No, absolutely not,' he said. 'Children need a lot of attention. They can be a strain on a strong marriage, let alone one that is suffering some teething problems.'

Her forehead creased again. 'So we were having some problems?'

Javier carefully considered how to answer. 'Very few relationships don't go through some sort of adjustment period. It was hard for both of us initially. I travel a great deal and you were new to my country and my language. In any case, it wasn't always convenient to take you with me because I like to concentrate on business when I am away. On the few occasions you did come with me, you were bored sitting around waiting for me. Some meetings go on and on until things are sorted out to everyone's satisfaction.'

'So I decided to stay at home and play the corporate wife role…' She chewed her lip again, as if the concept was totally foreign to her.

'Emilia.' He took her hand in his again, stroking the back of it with his thumb. 'It was the way things were between us. It was what we both wanted. You seemed happy with the arrangement when I asked you to marry me. You understood the rules. You were happy to play the game. You slipped into the role as if you were born to it.'

She looked at their joined hands, a sigh escaping from her lips. 'When I was a little girl I used to wish I could see into the future.' She looked back up into his gaze. 'But now I wish I could see into the past.'

He let her hand go and stood up from the bed. 'Sometimes the past is better left alone,' he said. 'It can't be changed.'

She pulled the sheet up to her chest, her forehead still creased in a frown. 'Will I see you before you leave tomorrow?' she asked.

He shook his head. 'I am leaving first thing.' He bent down and brushed his mouth against hers. *'Buenas noches.'*

'Buenas noches.' Her voice was a soft whisper that feathered its way down his spine as he left the room.

Aldana was in the kitchen when Emilia came downstairs the next morning. The atmosphere was distinctly chilly but she decided to ignore it. Ignore the bad, praise the good seemed the best way to handle a difficult person, she thought.

'Good morning, Aldana,' she said with a bright smile that she hoped didn't look too forced. 'It's a beautiful day, isn't it?'

The housekeeper sent her a reproachful look. 'I suppose as usual you will turn your nose up at the food I have set out for you?'

Emelia's smile fell away. 'Um…actually, I am quite hungry this morning,' she said. 'But you shouldn't have gone to any trouble.'

Aldana made a snorting noise and turned her attention to the bread she was making. 'I am paid to go to trouble,' she said. 'But it is a waste of my time and good food when people refuse to eat it.'

'I'm sorry if I've offended you in the past,' Emelia said after a tense silence. 'Would it help if I sat down with you and planned the week's menus? It would save you a lot of trouble and there would be less waste.'

Aldana dusted her hands on her apron in a dismissive fashion. 'You are not the right wife for Señor Mélendez,' she said. 'You do not love him as he deserves to be loved. You just love what he can give you.'

Emelia tried to disguise her shock at the housekeeper's blunt assessment by keeping her voice cool and controlled. 'You are entitled to your opinion but my relationship with my husband is no one's business but my own.'

Aldana gave another snort and turned her back to open the oven, signalling the end of the conversation.

Emelia decided to carry on as if things were normal, even though it troubled her deeply that the housekeeper thought her so unsuitable a wife for Javier. She had always imagined she would make a wonderful wife. After all, she had learned what not to do by watching first her parents' disastrous and volatile marriage, and then her father's subsequent ones after her mother had died. She had determined from a young age to marry for love and love only. Money and prestige would hold no sway with her. But now she wondered how closely she had clung to her ideals.

She ate a healthy breakfast of fruit and yogurt and toast and carried a cup of tea out to a sun-drenched terrace overlooking the villa's gardens.

The scenery was breathtaking and the fresh smell of recently cut grass teased her nostrils. Neatly trimmed box hedges created the more formal aspect of the garden, but beyond she could see colourful herbaceous borders and interesting pathways that led to various fountains or statues.

After she carried her cup back into the kitchen, Emelia went on a tour of the garden. The sun was warm but not overly so and a light breeze carried the delicate scent of late blooming roses to her. She stopped and picked one and, breathing in its fragrance, wondered how many times she had done exactly this. She poked the stem of the rose behind her ear and carried on, stopping at one of the fountains to watch the birds splashing and ruffling their feathers in the water.

The sound of a horse whinnying turned her head. In the distance Emelia could see a youth leading a magnificent looking stallion to what appeared to be a riding arena near the stables a little way from the villa. She walked back through the garden and made her way to where the youth was now lunging the horse on a lead rope. He was a powerful-looking animal with a proud head and flaring nostrils, his tail arched in defiance as his hooves pounded through the sand of the arena.

Emelia stood on the second rail of the fence so she could see over, watching as the stallion went through his paces. Without thinking, she spoke in Spanish to the youth. 'He's very temperamental, isn't he?'

'*Sí, señora,*' the youth answered. 'Your mare is much better mannered.'

Emelia looked at him blankly. 'I have a horse of my own?'

The youth looked at her as if she was *loca* but then he must have recalled what he had been told about her accident. '*Sí, señora,*' he said with a white toothed smile. 'She is in the stable. I exercised her earlier this morning.'

'Could I ride her, please?' Emelia asked.

He gave her a surprised look. 'You want to *ride* her?'

She nodded. 'Of course I do.'

'But you have never wanted to ride her before,' he said with a puzzled frown. 'You refused to even look at her.'

Emelia laughed off the suggestion. 'That's crazy. I love to ride. I had my own horse when my mother was alive. I used to spend every weekend and holidays at Pony Club or on riding camps.'

Pedro shrugged his shoulders as if he wasn't sure what to make of her as he made his way to the stables.

Emelia jumped down from the railing and followed him. 'I'm sorry but I've forgotten your name,' she said.

'Pedro,' he said. 'I look after the horses for Señor Mélendez. I have been working for him for two years now. The same time you have been married, *sí*?'

Emelia gave him a small smile, not sure how much he knew of her situation. The stallion snorted and pawed the ground and she stepped up to him and stroked his proud forehead. 'You are being a great big show-off, do you know that?' she crooned softly.

The stallion snorted again but then began to rub his head against her chest, almost pushing her over.

Pedro's look was still quizzical. 'He likes you, Señora Mélendez. But you used to be frightened of him. He is big and proud and has a mind of his own. He is…how you say…a softie inside.'

Emelia wondered if Pedro was talking about the horse or her husband. Probably both, she imagined. She breathed in the sweet smell of horse and hay and felt a flicker of something in her memory. She put a hand to her head, frowning as she tried to retrieve it before it disappeared.

'*Señora?*' Pedro's voice was concerned as he pulled the horse back from her. 'Are you all right? Did Gitano hurt you?'

'No, of course not,' Emelia said. 'I was just trying to remember something but it's gone now.'

Pedro led the stallion back to his stall and a short time later led out a pretty little mare. She had the same proud bearing as Gitano but her temperament was clearly very different. She whinnied when she caught sight of Emelia and her big soft round eyes shone with delight.

Emelia put her arms around the horse's neck, breathing in her sweet scent, closing her eyes as she searched her memory. A scene filtered through the fog in her head. It was a similar day to today, sunny with a light breeze. She was being led blindfolded down to the stables; she could even feel the nerves she had felt buzzing in the pit of her stomach. She could feel warm strong hands guiding her, a tall lean body brushing her from behind, the sharp citrus of his aftershave striking another chord of memory in her brain…

'*Señora Mélendez?*' Pedro's voice slammed the door on her memory. 'Are you all right?'

Emelia opened her eyes and, disguising her frustration, sent him a crooked smile. 'I'm fine,' she said.

'Callida looks very well. You must be doing a wonderful job of looking after her.'

'Señora,' Pedro said with rounded eyes, 'you remember her name, *sí*? Callida. Señor Mélendez bought her for you as a surprise for your birthday last month.'

Emelia stared at the youth for a moment, her brain whirling. 'I...I don't know how I remembered her name. It was just there in my head,' she said.

Pedro smiled a wide smile. 'It is good you are home. You will remember everything in time, *sí*?'

Emelia returned his smile but a little more cautiously. If only she had his confidence. But it did seem strange that Callida's name had been there on her tongue without her thinking about it; strange too that her Spanish had come to her equally as automatically. What else was lying inside her head, just waiting for the right trigger to unlock it?

Callida nudged against her, blowing at her through her velvet nostrils. Emelia tickled the horse's forelock. 'Can you saddle her for me?' she asked Pedro.

The lad's smile was quickly exchanged for a grave look. 'Señor Mélendez...I am not sure he would want you to ride. You have a head injury, *sí*? Not good to ride so soon.'

Emelia felt her neck and shoulders straighten in rebellion. 'I am perfectly well,' she said. 'And I would like to take Callida out to see if it helps me remember anything else. I need some exercise, in any case. I can't sit around all day doing nothing until my...hus...until Señor Mélendez returns.'

Pedro shifted his weight from foot to foot, his hands on Callida's leading rein fidgeting with agitation. 'I have been given instructions. I could lose my job.'

Emelia took the leading rein from him. 'I will explain to Señor Mélendez that I insisted. Don't worry. I won't let him fire you.'

The lad looked uncertain but Emelia had already made up her mind and led the mare to the stables. Pedro followed and, wordlessly and with tight lips, saddled the horse, handing Emelia a riding helmet once he had finished.

Emelia put it on and, giving him a smile, swung up into the saddle and rode out of the stable courtyard, re-lishing the sense of freedom it afforded her. She rode through the fields to the woods beyond, at a gentle walk at first and then, as her confidence grew, she squeezed Callida's sides to get her to trot. It wasn't long before she urged the horse into a canter, the rhythm so easy to ride to she felt as if she had been riding her for ever. How strange that Pedro had said she had refused to ride the horse Javier had bought for her. The horse was well bred and would have cost a mint. Why had she rejected such a beautiful precious gift?

After a while Emelia came to an olive grove and another flicker of memory was triggered in her brain. She slipped out of the saddle and led the horse to the spot where she thought the photograph she had seen in Javier's study was taken. Callida nudged against her and Emelia absently stroked the mare's neck as she looked at the soft green grass where she had lain with Javier. Had they made love under the shade of the olive trees? she wondered. Her skin tingled, the hairs on the back of her neck rising as she pictured them there, limbs en-tangled intimately, Javier's leanly muscled body pinning hers beneath the potent power of his.

She thought back to their conversation about the

terms of their marriage. The rules she had accepted supposedly without question. No children to tie either of them down. When had she decided she didn't want children? Had she said it just to keep Javier happy? He struck her as a man who valued and enjoyed his freedom. In many ways he seemed to still live the life of a playboy: regular international travel on private jets, a disposable income, no ties or responsibilities other than a relatively new wife who apparently didn't travel with him with any regularity. Children would definitely require a commitment from him he might not feel ready to agree to at this stage of his life.

Emelia, on the other hand, had always loved children; it was one of the reasons she had wanted to teach instead of perform. She loved their innocence and their wonder at the world and had always dreamed of having a family of her own some day. Growing up as an only child with numerous stepmothers entering and exiting her life had made her determined to marry a man who would be a wonderful husband and father, a man who was faithful and steadfast, nothing at all like her restless father. Why then had she married a man who didn't want the same things she did? Surely she hadn't slept with him for any other reason than love. She had vowed ever since her disastrous affair of the past that she would never make that mistake again. But, thinking about the current of electricity that had flared between her and Javier from the first moment he had stepped up to her bedside in the hospital, Emelia had to wonder if she had fallen victim to the power of sexual attraction after all. If only Peter was still alive so she could ask him to fill in the gaps for her.

She had made a couple of girlfriends at the hotel but

none of them were particularly close. Besides, they had been on temporary visas and would have moved on by now. It seemed the only way to find out her past was piece by piece, like putting a complicated jigsaw puzzle back together without the original picture as a guide.

Emelia rode back to the villa and handed Callida over to Pedro, who had very obviously been hovering about, waiting for her return. He took the mare with visible relief and reluctantly agreed on having the horse ready for another ride at the same time tomorrow.

When Emelia came downstairs after a shower she was informed by Aldana she had a visitor.

'She is waiting in *la sala*,' the housekeeper said with a frosty look.

'*Gracias*, Aldana,' Emelia said. 'But who is it? Someone I should know?'

Aldana pursed her lips but, before she could respond, female footsteps click-clacked from behind Emelia and a young voice called out, 'So you are back.'

Emelia turned to see a young female version of Javier stalking haughtily towards her. The young woman's dark-as-night eyes were flashing, her mouth was a thin line of disapproval and her long raven hair practically bristled with anger. 'Izabella?'

The young woman's eyes narrowed to paper-thin slits. 'So you remember me, do you? How very interesting.'

Emelia took a steadying breath. 'It was a guess, but apparently a very good one.'

Izabella planted her hands on her boyishly slim hips, sending Emelia another wish-you-were-dead glare. 'You shouldn't be here. You have no right to be here after what you did.'

Emelia marshalled her defences, keeping her tone civil but determined. 'I'm not sure what I am supposedly guilty of doing. Perhaps you could enlighten me.'

Izabella tossed her glossy dark head. 'Don't play the innocent with me. It might have worked with my brother but it won't work with me. I know what you are up to.'

Emelia was conscious of the housekeeper listening to every word. 'Would you like to come into *la sala* and discuss this further?' she asked.

Izabella gave another flash of her midnight eyes. 'I don't care who hears what I have to say.'

'Does your brother know you are here?' Emelia asked after a tense pause.

The young woman's haughty stance slipped a notch. 'He is not my keeper,' she said, making a moue of her mouth.

'That's not what he told me,' Emelia returned.

Izabella gave her head another toss as she folded her arms across her chest. 'He wouldn't have taken you back, you know. He only did it because he had no choice. The press would have crucified him if he'd divorced you so soon after the accident.'

Emelia felt as if a heavy weight had landed on her chest. She felt faint and had to struggle to remain steady on her feet. She would have excused herself but her desire to know more about her forgotten marriage overruled any concern for her well-being. 'Wh-what are you saying?'

'He was going to divorce you,' Izabella said with an aristocratic hoist of her chin. 'He had already contacted his lawyer.'

Emelia moistened her lips. 'On…on what grounds?'

Izabella's gaze was pure venom. 'Adultery.' She almost spat the word at Emelia. 'You ran away to be with your lover.'

Emelia stood in a frozen silence as she mentally replayed every conversation she'd had with Javier since she had woken in the hospital. While he hadn't accused her of anything openly, he had alluded to what the press had made of her relationship with Peter. He had also expressed his bitterness at her remembering Peter while not remembering him, which she had thought was a reasonable reaction under the circumstances. But if Javier truly believed her to have been unfaithful, what was he waiting for? Why not divorce her and be done with it? Did he really care what the press would make of it? What did he hope to gain by taking her back as if nothing had happened? It didn't make sense, not unless he loved her and was prepared to leave the past in the past, but somehow she didn't think that was the case. He desired her. She was acutely aware of the heat of his gaze every time it rested on her, indeed as aware of her own response to him. She was not immune to him, in spite of her memory loss. One kiss had shown how vulnerable she was to him.

'But it's not true,' she said after a moment. 'I didn't commit adultery.'

Izabella rolled her eyes. 'Of course you would say that. Your lover is dead, so what else could you do? You had to come back to Javier. He is rich and you had nowhere else to go. Even your own father would not take you back. You are nothing but a gold-digger.'

Emelia felt ill but worked hard to hold her composure. 'Look, Izabella, I realise you must be upset if you have heard rumours such as the outrageous one you just relayed to me, but I can assure you I have never been unfaithful to your brother. It's just not something I would do. I know it in my heart.'

Izabella gave her a challenging glare. 'How would you know? You say you don't remember anything from the past two years. How do you know *what* you did?'

It was a very good point, Emelia had to admit. But, deep down, she knew she would never have betrayed her marriage vows. How she was going to prove it was something she had yet to work out. Her reputation had been ruined by scandalous reports in the media. Who would believe her, even if she could remember what had happened that fateful day?

'Did you ever love my brother?' Izabella asked.

The question momentarily knocked Emelia off course. She looked at the young woman blankly, knowing as each pulsing second passed another layer of blame was being shovelled on top of her. 'I…I don't feel it is anyone's business but Javier's and mine,' she said.

Izabella gave a scathing snort. 'You never loved him. What you love is what he can give you—the lifestyle, the clothes, the jewellery. It's all you have ever wanted from him.'

'That is not true.' *Please don't let it be true*, Emelia thought.

'He is not going to remain faithful to you, you know. Why should he when you played up behind his back?'

Emelia felt a stake go through her middle. It surprised her how much Izabella's coolly delivered statement hurt her. Her mind filled with images of Javier with other women, his body locked with theirs, giving and receiving pleasure. Perhaps even now he was entertaining himself with some gorgeous creature in

Moscow. She shook her head, trying to get the torturous images to disappear. 'No,' she said in a rasping whisper. 'No…'

'He should never have married you,' Izabella said. 'Everyone told him it would end in disaster.'

Emelia lifted her aching head to meet Izabella's gaze. 'Why did he marry me, then?'

'Because he needed to be married to gain access to our father's estate,' Izabella said.

Emelia felt her heart give another sickening lurch. 'He married me to…to get *money*?'

'You surely don't think he loved you, do you?' Izabella threw her a disdainful look. 'He wanted you and what he wants he usually gets. You were a convenient wife. A trophy he wanted by his side. But that is all you are to him. He does not love you.'

'Did I *know* this?' Emelia asked in a hoarse whisper.

Izabella's expression lost some of its hauteur. 'I am not sure…' She bit down on her bottom lip in a way that seemed to strip years off her. 'Perhaps not. Maybe I shouldn't have said anything…'

Emelia reached for something to hold onto to steady herself. 'I can't believe I agreed to such an emotionless arrangement…' She looked at the young girl with an anguished expression on her face. 'I always wanted to marry for love. Are you sure I was not in love with Javier?'

Izabella looked troubled. 'If you were, you never said anything to me. You kept your feelings to yourself, although it was pretty obvious you were attracted to him. But then he's attractive to a lot of women.'

Emelia didn't want to think about that. It was just too painful. 'I'm sorry if I've given you the wrong impression,' she said after a moment. 'Javier told me you and I haven't had the easiest of relationships. I hope I haven't done anything to upset you. I have never had a sister before. I've always wanted one, especially after my mother died. It would have been nice to have someone to talk to about girl stuff.'

Izabella's dark brown eyes softened a fraction. 'Javier is the best brother a girl could have but there are times when I would rather share what is going on in my life with another woman. My mother is OK but she just worries if I talk to her about boys. She always thinks I am going to get pregnant or something.'

Emelia smiled. 'I guess it's what mothers do best— worry.'

Izabella's mouth tilted in a wary smile. 'You seem so different,' she said. 'Almost like a completely different person.'

'To tell you the truth, Izabella, I feel like a completely different person from the one everyone expects me to be,' Emelia confessed. 'I look at the clothes in my wardrobe and I can't believe I have ever worn them. They seem so…so…I don't know…not me. And when I was down at the stables Pedro told me I had refused to ride the horse Javier bought me last month for my birthday. I don't understand it. Why would I not ride that beautiful horse?'

'Ever since your birthday you seemed a little unsettled,' Izabella said. 'When you had the accident we all assumed it was because you were in love with another man. Now, I wonder if it wasn't because you were becoming a little tired of your life here. There is only so much time you can spend in the shops or the gym.'

Emelia felt her face heat up with colour. 'Yes, well,

that's another thing I don't get. I *hate* the gym. I can think of nothing worse than an elliptical trainer or a stationary bike and weight machines.'

'You worked out religiously,' Izabella said. 'You lost pounds and pounds within weeks of meeting Javier. And you are always dieting whenever Javier's away.'

Emelia thought back to her hearty breakfast that morning. 'No wonder I've been such a pain to be around,' she said with a wry grimace. 'I'm hopeless at diets. I have no self control. I get bitchy when I deprive myself.'

Izabella grinned. 'I do too.'

There was a little pause.

'You won't tell Javier I was so horrible to you, will you?' Izabella said with a worried look. 'He will be angry with me for upsetting you. I should have thought… You have just had a terrible accident. I am sorry about your friend. You must be very sad.'

'I am coping with it,' Emelia said. 'But I wish I knew what really happened that day.'

Izabella bit her lip again. 'Maybe you were leaving Javier because you didn't want to continue with the marriage as it was. The press would have latched on to it pretty quickly and made it out to be something it wasn't. Javier was furious. He was determined to divorce you but then he got news of the accident.' Her slim throat rose and fell. 'He was devastated when he heard you might not make it. He tried to hide it but I could tell he was terrified you would die.'

Emelia frowned as she tried to make sense of it all. If Javier didn't want her in his life permanently, why suffer her presence just because of her memory loss? Given what he believed of her, what hope did she have of restoring his trust in her? Had he known her so little that he had readily believed the specious rumours of the press? What sort of marriage had they had that it would crumble so quickly? Surely over the almost two years they had been together a level of trust had been established? She felt sure she would not have settled for anything else. It was so frustrating to have no way of finding out the truth. Her mind was like the missing black box of a crashed aircraft. Within it were all the clues to what had happened and until it was found she would have to try and piece together what she could to make sense of it all. Her head ached from the pressure of trying to remember. Her eyes felt as if they had been stabbed with roofing nails, pain pulsed from her temples like hammer blows.

Izabella touched Emelia on the arm. 'You are very pale,' she said. 'Is there anything I can ask Aldana to get for you?'

'I don't think Aldana will appreciate having to act as nursemaid to me,' Emelia said, putting a hand to her throbbing temple. 'She doesn't seem to like me very much.'

'She has never liked you but it's probably not your fault,' Izabella said. 'Her daughter once had a fling with Javier. It wasn't serious but, ever since, Aldana has been convinced no one but her daughter was good enough for Javier. I think you tried hard at first to get along but after a while you gave up.'

It explained a lot, Emelia thought. She couldn't imagine being deliberately rude to the household staff under any circumstances. But perhaps she had lost patience with Aldana, as Izabella had suggested, and consequently acted like the spoilt, overly indulged trophy wife everyone assumed her to be. 'I am so glad you came here today,' she said. 'I hope we can be friends.'

'I would like that very much,' Izabella said and, looking sheepish, added, 'I haven't always treated you very well. You were so beautiful and accomplished, so talented at playing the piano. I was such a cow to you, I guess because I was jealous. I probably contributed to your unhappiness with Javier.'

'I am sure you had no part to play in that at all,' Emelia said. 'I should have been more mature and understanding.'

'Please, you must promise not to tell Javier I was rude to you before,' Izabella said. 'I am so ashamed of myself.'

'You have no need to be,' Emelia said. 'Anyway, you were only acting out of your concern for him.'

Izabella's gaze melted. 'Yes, he's a wonderful brother. He would do anything for me. I am very lucky to have him.'

'He's lucky to have you,' Emelia said, thinking of all of her years alone, without anyone to stand up for her. It seemed nothing had changed: this recent scandal demonstrated how truly alone she was. No one had challenged the rumours. No one had defended her.

Izabella suddenly cocked her head. 'Your memory must be coming back, Emelia,' she said with an engaging grin.

Emelia shook her head. 'No, I've tried and tried but I can't remember much at all.'

'Except Spanish.'

Emelia felt her heart knock against her ribcage. She

hadn't realised until that point that every word she had
exchanged with Izabella had been in Spanish.

Every single word.

CHAPTER SIX

IZABELLA had arranged to join some friends in Valencia the following day before she flew back to Paris so Emelia was left to her own devices. After a shower and breakfast, she wandered out into the gardens, stopping every now and again to pick a rose until, after half an hour, her arms were nearly full. She went back to the villa and laid them down on one of the large kitchen benches, breathing in the delicate fragrance as she searched for some vases.

Aldana appeared just as Emelia was carrying a vase full of blooms into *la sala*. 'What are you doing?' she asked, frowning formidably.

'I picked some roses,' Emelia said. 'I thought they would look nice in some of the rooms to brighten them up a bit. I hope you don't mind.'

Aldana took the vase out of Emelia's grasp. 'Señor Mélendez does not like roses in the house,' she said in a clipped tone.

Emelia felt her shoulders slump. 'Oh…sorry, I didn't realise…'

The housekeeper shot her another hateful glare as she carried the roses out of the room. The look seemed to suggest that, in Aldana's opinion, Emelia had never known her husband's likes and dislikes like a proper loving wife should do.

Emelia let out a sigh once she was alone. There was a baby grand piano at one end of *la sala*, positioned out of the direct sunlight from the windows. She went over to it and sat down and after a moment she opened the lid and ran her fingers over the keys, trying to remember what song she had played the night she had met Javier, but it was like trying to play a new piece without the musical score. She played several pieces, hoping that one would unlock her mind, but none did. She closed the lid in frustration and left the room to make her way down to the stables.

Pedro had Callida saddled for her when she arrived but he looked disgruntled. 'Señor Mélendez will not be happy about this,' he said. 'He told all the staff to watch out for you, to make sure you do not come to any harm while he is away.'

'Señor Mélendez is several thousand kilometres away,' Emelia said as she swung up into the saddle. 'While the cat's away this little mouse is going to do what she wants.'

Pedro stepped back from the horse with a disapproving frown. 'He sometimes comes back early from his trips abroad,' he said. 'He expects his staff to act the same whether he is here or not. He trusts us.'

But not me, Emelia thought resentfully as she rode off. No doubt he had only put his staff on watch over her to see that she didn't stray too far from the boundaries of the villa. His solicitous care had nothing to do with any deep feelings on his part. He wanted to keep her a virtual prisoner until the press interest died down. After that, who knew what he planned to do? All she knew was his plans would probably not include her being in his life for the long term.

As enjoyable as the ride was, it didn't unearth any clues to her past. She came back to the stables an hour and a half later, fighting off a weighty despondency. The olive grove today had simply been an olive grove. No further memories surfaced. Nothing struck a chord of familiarity.

Disappointment and frustration continued to sour her mood as she walked back to the villa through the gardens. She felt hot and sticky so when she came across a secluded section of the garden where an infinity pool was situated, she decided to take advantage of the sparkling blue water and the warmth of the afternoon.

Rummaging through the walk-in wardrobe in search of swimwear was another revelation to her. Naturally modest, she found it hard to believe she wore any of the skimpy bikinis she found in one of the drawers. There were pink ones and red ones and yellow ones and ones with polka dots, a black one with silver diamantés and a white one with gold circles in between the triangles of fabric that would barely cover her breasts, let alone her lower body. In the end she chose the red one as it was the least revealing, although once she had it on and checked her appearance in the full length mirrors she was glad Javier was not expected home. She might as well have been naked.

The water was warmed by the sun but still refreshing enough to make Emelia swim length after length without exhaustion. She wondered how many times she had done this, stroking her way through the water, perhaps with Javier swimming alongside her, or his long legs tangling with hers as he kissed or caressed her. In spite of the warmth of the pool and the sun, Emelia felt her skin lift in little goosebumps the more she let her mind wander about what had occurred in the past.

As she surfaced at the end of the pool she saw a long pair of trouser-clad legs, the large male feet encased in expensive-looking leather shoes. Her heart gave a stop-start as her eyes moved upwards to meet the coal-black gaze of Javier.

'I thought I might find you here,' he said.

Emelia pushed her hair out of her face, conscious of her barely clad breasts just at the water's level. 'I didn't realise you would be back. I thought you were coming home tomorrow.'

He tugged at his tie as his gaze held hers. 'I managed to get through the work and flew back ahead of schedule.'

Emelia swallowed as she saw him toss his tie to one of the sun loungers. His fingers began undoing the buttons of his business shirt, one by one, each opening revealing a little more of his muscular chest. 'Um… what are you doing?' she said.

'I thought I might join you,' he said, shrugging himself out of his shirt, tossing it in the same direction as his tie, his dark eyes still tethering hers.

She watched in a spellbound stasis as his hands went to his belt, slipping it through the waistband of his trousers, casting it on top of his shirt and tie. The sound of his zip going down jolted her out of her trance. 'Y-you're surely not going to swim without bathers…are you?'

A corner of his mouth lifted. 'Do you have any objection, *querida*?' he asked.

Emelia could think of several but she couldn't seem to get her voice to work. She stood in the water as he heeled himself out of his shoes and purposefully pulled off his socks. Her heart started thumping irregularly as he stepped out of his trousers, leaving him in close-fitting black briefs that left almost nothing to her imagination. She felt a stirring deep and low in her belly. He was so potently male, so powerfully built, lean but muscular at the same time, hair in all the right places, marking him as different from her as could be. His skin was a deep olive, tanned by the sun, each rippling ridge of his abdomen like coils of steel. Her fingertips suddenly itched to explore every hard contour of him, to feel the satin quality of his skin and unleash the latent power of his body. She wondered if her attraction was a new thing or an old thing. Was her body remembering what her mind could or would not? How else could she explain this unbelievable tension she felt when he was near her? She had never felt like this with anyone before. It was as if he awakened everything that was female in her body, making her long to discover the power of the passion his glittering dark gaze promised.

Being at the shallower end, he didn't dive into the water; instead, he slipped in with an agility that made Emelia aware of every plane of his body as the water his entry displaced washed against her. It was as if he had touched her; the water felt just like an intimate caress: smooth, gentle, cajoling, tempting. Her eyes were still locked with his; she couldn't seem to move out of the magnetic range of his dark-as-night eyes. They burned, they seared and they smouldered as he closed the distance between their bodies, stopping just in front of her, not quite touching but close enough for her to feel the pull of his body through the weight of the water.

'Why so shy?' he asked.

Emelia licked a droplet of water off her lips. 'Um…I know this is probably something you…I mean we have done lots of times but I…I…feel too exposed.'

His lips slanted in a smile. 'You got rid of your timidity a long time ago, Emelia. We skinny-dipped together all the time.'

She felt the pit of her stomach tilt. 'But surely someone could have seen us?'

He gave a little couldn't-care-less shrug. 'The pool area is private. In any case, what would it matter if someone had seen us? We are married and this is private property. It is not as if we were doing anything wrong.'

Emelia chewed at her lip, wishing she could download all her memories so she wasn't feeling so lost and uncertain. While she had been dressing in the bikini earlier she had seen from her lightly tanned skin that she had been in the sun and not always with all her clothes on. She had not been the type to sunbathe topless in the past, but then two whole years of her life were missing. Who knew what she had grown comfortable with over that time? It made her feel all the more on edge around Javier. He knew far more about her than she knew about him. And yet she could sense in her body a growing recognition that flickered a little more each time they were together.

'Aldana told me you had a visitor while I was away,' Javier said.

Emelia kept her expression masked. 'Yes. Izabella called in. She's gone to stay with friends in Valencia before she goes back to Paris.'

'Did you recognise her?'

She shook her head. 'No, but I soon figured out who she was. She is very like you. It is obvious you are related. You have the same hair and eyes.'

'I hope you refrained from getting into an argument with her,' he said, still holding her gaze. 'I would not want either of you upset.'

'No, we didn't argue,' Emelia said. 'I found her to be friendly and pleasant and not in the least hostile. She's a very beautiful and poised young woman. You must be very proud of her.'

He frowned as he studied her through narrowed eyes. 'What did you talk about?'

'The usual girl stuff,' she said. 'We have a lot in common, actually.'

'She is a little headstrong at times,' he admitted. 'But then she is still young.'

Emelia went to move to the steps leading out of the pool but he placed a hand on her arm, stopping her from moving away from him. 'Where are you going?' he asked.

'I'm getting cold,' she said. 'I want to have a shower.'

He cupped both of her shoulders with his hands. 'No kiss for my return?'

Emelia felt her eyes widen and her stomach did another flip turn. 'It's not as if things are the same…as before,' she said. 'I need more time.'

Something moved at the back of his eyes. 'I think the sooner we slip back into our previous routine the better,' he said. 'I am convinced it will help you remember.'

'You're assuming I will remember,' she said. 'I had no such assurance from any of the doctors or therapists at the hospital.'

His hands tightened as soon as he felt her try to escape again. 'It doesn't matter if you remember or not. It doesn't change the fact that we are married.'

Emelia straightened her spine in defiance but, by doing so, it brought her pelvis into direct contact with his. The hot hard heat of him was like being zapped with a thousand volts of electricity. She felt the tingles shoot through her from head to foot. His eyes dropped to the startled 'O' of her mouth and then, as if in slow motion, gradually lowered his head until his lips sealed hers.

It was a slow burn of a kiss, heating her to her core as each pulsing second passed. His tongue probed the seam of her mouth for entry and she gave it on a whimper of pleasure. The rasp of his tongue as it mated with hers sent a cascading shiver down the backs of her legs and up again, right to the back of her neck. She felt her toes curl on the tiled floor of the pool as his kiss deepened. His arms had gone from the tops of her shoulders down the slim length of her arms to settle about her waist, holding her against his pelvis, leaving her acutely aware of his rock-hard arousal. Her body responded automatically, the ache between her thighs becoming more insistent the firmer he held her against him. She moved against him, a slight nudge at first and then a blatant rub to feel the pleasure his body offered.

He slowly but surely walked her backwards, his thighs brushing hers with each step, his mouth still locked on her mouth, his body jammed tight against her. His hands moved up from her waist to deftly untie the strings of her bikini. It fell away, leaving her breasts free for his touch. She drew in a sharp breath as his hands cupped her, his thumb gently stroking over each nipple, making her flesh cry out for more. His mouth left hers and went on a leisurely mission, exploring every dip and curve on the way down to her breasts: the sensitive pleasure spots behind each of her earlobes, the hollows above her collarbone and the super-reactive skin of her neck. She tilted her head to one side as he nibbled and nipped in turn, her belly turning over in delight as he finally made his way to her breasts. He left her nipples alone this time and concentrated instead on the sensitive under curves of each breast, first with his fingers and then with the heat and fire of his mouth. She arched up against him, wanting more, wanting it all, wanting to feel whatever he had made her feel in the past.

His mouth came back to her searching, hungry one, his hands going to the strings holding her bikini bottom in place. Emelia's hands moved from around his neck to the small of his back, delighting in the way he groaned deeply as he surged against her. Casting inhibition aside, she peeled away his briefs, freeing him into her hands. She felt a hitch in her breath as she shaped his steely length, the throb of his blood pounding against her fingers. He was so thick with desire it made her own blood race at the thought of him moving inside her.

He tore his mouth off hers, looking down at her with eyes glittering with desire. 'You have certainly not forgotten how to drive me wild with wanting you,' he said. 'How about it, *querida*? Shall we finish this here and now, or wait for later?'

Emelia felt the cold slap of shock bring her back to reality. What was she doing allowing him such liberties and outside where anyone could see if they put their mind to it? And what was she doing touching him as if she wanted him to finish what he had started? What was wrong with her? Surely she had not become such a

slave of the flesh? She had always abhorred such irre-
sponsible behaviour amongst her peers; the casual
approach to sex was something she had never gone in
for. She put up her chin, working hard to maintain her
composure when she was stark naked. 'What makes you
so sure I would give my consent, here or anywhere?'

His smile was on the edge of mocking. 'Because I
know you, Emelia. I know how you respond to me. A
couple of minutes more and you would have been
begging for it.'

There was nothing figurative about the slap Emelia
landed on the side of Javier's face. It jerked his head
back, made his nostrils flare and his mouth tighten to a
flat line of tension. 'You know, you really shouldn't
have done that,' he said with a coolness she was sure he
was nowhere near feeling.

Emelia refused to wilt under his hard black gaze.
'You insulted me. You practically called me a wanton
tramp.'

One of his hands rubbed at the red hand-sized mark
on his jaw. 'So if someone allegedly insults you it's OK
to use violence?' he asked.

She bit the inside of her mouth, suddenly ashamed
of how she had reacted, but there was no way she was
going to apologise to him. She turned and searched for
her bikini, struggling to put it back on while still in the
water. She was conscious of Javier's eyes following her
every movement and her resentment and anger
hardened like a golf ball-sized lump in the middle of her
chest. Once she was covered, she stomped up the pool
steps, snatching up her towel on the way past the sun
lounger where she had left it.

* * *

The moment Emelia came out of the en suite bathroom after a lengthy shower she knew something was amiss. Her eyes went to the bed where a black leather brief-case was lying at the foot of it. She heard the sound of someone moving about in the walk-in wardrobe and, clutching her bathrobe a little tighter, spun around to find Aldana coming out with some spare coat hangers.

'What's going on?' Emelia asked in Spanish.

The housekeeper gave her a pursed-lipped look. 'Señor Mélendez instructed me to hang his clothes.'

Emelia's eyes widened in alarm. 'What? In...in *here*?'

Aldana gave a shrug as she walked past. 'It is none of my business what he wants or why. I just do as I am told. He wanted me to bring his things back in here where they belong.'

The housekeeper left before Emelia could respond and within seconds Javier strode in. She turned on him, her eyes flashing with fury. *'Qué diablos está pasando?'* she asked. 'What the hell is going on?'

He stood very still for a moment before responding in Spanish. 'I could ask you the very same thing. What the hell *is* going on? Especially as it seems at least some part of your memory has returned without you telling me.'

Emelia felt her cheeks fill with colour. 'I...I was going to tell you...'

'When did it happen?' he asked.

She could barely hold his gaze as she confessed. 'I found myself understanding it and speaking it from the start. I don't know why. It was just...there.'

'How convenient.'

Emelia's hands tightened where they clutched the

neckline of her bathrobe. 'I know what you're thinking but it's not true. I don't remember anything else. I swear to you.'

He gave her a cynical smile that contained no trace of amusement. 'I met Pedro the stable boy on my way in earlier,' he said. 'He was full of excitement over how you remembered your mare's name without any prompting from him.'

Emelia pressed her lips together. 'I forgot I remembered...' It sounded as stupid as she felt and she lowered her gaze from the hard probe of his, hating herself for blushing.

'He also told me you have finally ridden your horse,' he said.

'I can't explain why I never rode Callida before.' She looked up at him again. 'You must have been very annoyed with me after spending so much money on such a beautiful animal.'

He held her gaze for a long moment. 'It wasn't the first present you rejected of late,' he said. 'It seemed over the last few weeks nothing I did for you or bought for you could please you.'

Emelia wondered if she had been hankering after more from him than what money could buy. It seemed much more in line with her true character. She had been given expensive gifts for most of her life but they hadn't made her feel any more secure.

Javier used two fingers to lift her chin, searing her gaze with his. 'I want you to tell me the moment you remember anything else, do you understand? I don't care what time of day it is or if I am away or here. Just tell me.'

She let out an uneven breath as she stepped out from

under his hold. 'You can't force me to remember you, Javier. It doesn't happen like that. I read up about it. Sometimes the memories are blocked because of trauma, either physical or emotional or maybe even both.'

A muscle worked in his jaw, the silence stretching and stretching like a threadbare piece of elastic.

'So what you are saying is you might be subconsciously blocking all memory of our life together?' he finally said.

Emelia released her bottom lip from the savaging of her teeth. 'I'm not sure if that's what has happened or not,' she said. 'Was there something that happened that might have caused me to do that? Something deeply upsetting, I mean.'

The silence stretched again, even further this time.

'I was away the day you left for London,' Javier said heavily. He waited a beat before continuing. 'I had only just come back from Moscow when we had an argument. I flew straight back afterwards.'

Emelia felt a frown tugging at her forehead. 'What did we argue about?'

His eyes met hers briefly before moving away to focus on a point beyond her left shoulder. 'The papers had printed some rubbish about me being involved with someone in Russia, a nightclub singer.'

Emelia felt a fist wrap itself around her heart. 'Was it…was it true?'

His dark eyes flashed with irritation as they came back to hers. 'Of course it wasn't true. I have to deal with those rumours all the time. I thought you were OK about it. We'd talked about it early in our marriage. We used to laugh about some of the stuff that was printed.

I warned you what it would be like, that there would be constant rumours, often set off by business rivals.'

He stopped to scrape a hand through his hair. 'But this time for some reason you refused to accept my explanation. You got it in your head that I was playing up behind your back. It seemed nothing I said would change your mind.'

'So we had an argument…'

'Yes,' he said. 'I'm afraid it was a bit of an ugly scene.'

Emelia raised her brows questioningly. 'How ugly?'

He let out a long tense breath. 'There was a lot of shouting and name calling. We were both angry and upset. I should have cut the argument short but I was annoyed because you seemed determined to want our marriage to be something it was never intended to be.'

Emelia sent him a let's-see-if-you-can-deny-this look. 'So apparently I wasn't too happy you had married me to gain access to your father's estate, right?'

His dark gaze turned flinty. 'That was one of the things we argued about, yes. While I was away, my father's mistress had rung you and filled your head with that and other such nonsense to get back at me. But the truth is my reasons for marrying you had very little to do with my father's will.'

She rolled her eyes in disbelief. 'Oh, come now, Javier. You talk of our marriage as some sort of business proposal, rules and regulations and me suddenly stepping outside of them. What the hell was the point of being married if not because we loved each other?'

'Love was not part of the deal,' he said, shocking Emelia into silence. 'I wanted a wife. Some of the business people I deal with are old-fashioned and conservative in their views. They feel more comfortable dealing with a man in a seemingly stable relationship. I know it sounds a little cold-blooded but you were quite happy to take on the corporate wife role. We were ideally matched physically. It was all I wanted from you and you from me.'

She stood looking at him with her emotions reeling. How could she have agreed to such a marriage? A relationship based on sex and nothing else? Had she turned into a clone of her father's set, in spite of her determination not to? She had become a trophy wife, an exotic bird in a gilded cage. Indulged and pampered until her mind went numb.

Javier let out another breath and sent his hand through his hair again. 'Emelia…' He hesitated for a moment before he continued. 'You might not remember it but we made love during that last argument.'

Emelia felt her brows lift again but remained silent.

His gaze remained steady on hers. 'In hindsight, it was perhaps not the best way to leave things between us. There was so much left unresolved. I have had cause to wonder if that is why you rushed off to London the way you did.'

Emelia searched her mind for some trace of that scene but nothing came to her. 'Did I explain why I left? In a note or something?'

'Yes,' he said.

Hope flickered in her chest. 'Can I see it?'

'I tore it into shreds,' he said, his mouth tightening at the memory. 'I got home from Moscow two days after you left. That is another thing I am not particularly proud of. I should have come straight to London as soon as I knew you were there. I was packing a bag when I got the call about the accident.'

'What did I say in the note?' Emelia asked.

He looked at her silently for several moments. 'You said you were leaving me, that you no longer wanted to continue with our marriage. You wanted out.'

Emelia rubbed at her forehead, as if that would unlock the memories stored inside her head. OK, so she had been leaving him. That much was pretty certain. Was it because she had become tired of their shallow relationship, as Izabella had suggested? Emelia knew she must have been very unhappy to have come to that decision. Unhappy or desperate. 'The rumours…' she said. 'You mentioned a few days ago there was some speculation about my relationship with Peter Marshall. Did you afford me the same level of trust you expected of me, in similar if not the same circumstances?'

He visibly tensed; all of his muscles seemed to contract as if sprayed with fast setting glue. 'I am the first to admit that I was jealous of your relationship with him,' he said, biting each word out from between his clenched teeth. 'He seemed at great pains whenever I was around to show me just how close you were. He was always touching you, slinging an arm around your waist or shoulders. It made me want to lash out.'

Emelia frowned at his vehement confession. 'Peter was a touchy-feely sort of person. It was just his way. I am sure I would have told you that right from the start.'

His eyes flashed with heat. 'You did, but it still annoyed the hell out of me.'

He was jealous. He hated admitting it, Emelia was sure, but he was positively vibrating with it. She could see it in the way he held himself, his hands clenching and unclenching as if he wanted to hit something.

He paced the room a couple of times before he came back to stand in front of her. 'If I was wrong about your relationship with Marshall then I am sorry,' he said. 'All the evidence pointed to you being guilty of an affair, but in hindsight there are probably numerous explanations for why you were in that car with him.'

Emelia felt a weight come off her shoulders. 'You truly believe I wasn't unfaithful?'

He held her look for endless seconds. 'Let's just let it go,' he said on a long breath. 'I don't want to be reminded of the mistakes I have made in the past. We have to concentrate on the here and now. I want to see you get well again. I feel it is my fault you were almost killed. I cannot forgive myself for driving you away in such an emotionally charged state. I should have insisted we sit down and sort things out like two rational adults. Instead, I let business take precedence, hoping things would settle down by the time I got back.'

Emelia stood looking at him in silence. His gruff admission of guilt stirred her deep inside. She could tell it was unfamiliar territory for him. He didn't seem the type to readily admit when he was in the wrong.

She breathed in the clean male scent of him as he stood so broodingly before her. He had showered and changed into a polo shirt and casual trousers. His hair was still damp, ink-black and curling at the ends where it needed a trim. She wanted to run her hands through it the way she used to do... She jolted as if he had struck her, staring up at him, her heart beating like a hyperactive hammer.

'What's wrong?' he asked, taking her by the shoulders.

She looked up into his face, frowning as she tried to focus on the sliver of memory that had made its way through. As if by their own volition, her hands went to his hair, her fingers playing with the silky strands in slow, measured strokes. She saw his throat move up and down and, glancing at his mouth, she felt another tiny flicker of recognition. Her right hand went to his lips, her fingers tracing over the tense line, again and again until it finally softened, the slight rasp of his evening shadow as she stroked the leanness of his jaw, the only sound, apart from their breathing, in the silence.

'Emelia—' his voice was low and deep and scratchy '—what have you remembered?'

She looked into his dark eyes. 'Your hair…I remembered running my fingers through it…lots and lots of times… It's longer now, isn't it?'

'Yes, I've been too busy to get it cut.' His grip on her shoulders tightened and his eyes were intense as they held hers. 'Can you remember anything else?' he asked.

'I'm not sure…' Emelia tried to focus again. 'It was just a fleeting thing. Like a flashback or something.'

His hands slipped down from her shoulders to encircle her wrists, his thumbs absently stroking her. 'Don't force it. It will come when it wants to. We have to be patient.' He let out a rough sounding sigh and added ruefully, '*I* have to be patient.'

Emelia felt the drugging warmth of his touch on the undersides of her wrists. Her blood leapt in her veins and she wondered if he could feel the way he affected her. Her belly was turning into a warm pool of longing, her legs unsteady as his eyes came to hers, holding them for a pulsing moment.

Time seemed to slow and then stand impossibly still.

Without a word, he lifted one of his hands to the curve of her cheek, cupping her face gently, his thumb moving back and forth in a mesmerising touch that seemed to stroke away every single reason why she should ease back out of his embrace. Instead, she found herself stepping closer, her body touching his from chest to thigh, feeling the stirring of his body against her, the hot hard heat of him lighting a fire that she now realised had smouldered within her from the moment she had woken up in the hospital and encountered his dark unreadable gaze.

'Emelia.'

The way he said her name was her undoing. Low and deep, an urgency in the uttering of the syllables, a need that she could feel resonating in her own body, like a tuning fork being struck too hard, humming, vibrating and quivering with want.

She lifted her mouth to the slow descent of his, her arms snaking around his middle, her breasts pressed up against his hard chest, a feeling, as his lips sealed hers and his hands cradled her head, that she had finally come home…

CHAPTER SEVEN

EMELIA sighed with pleasure as Javier's mouth urged hers into a heated response. Desire was like a punch, hitting her hard as his tongue deftly searched for hers. He found it, toyed with it, stroking and stabbing, calling it into a dance that mimicked what was to come. Her body felt as if spot fires had been set all through it, the blood raced and thundered in her veins as his kiss grew all the more insistent, all the more hotly sensual. The delicate network of nerves in her core twanged with need, her breasts tightened and tingled where they were pressed against him, and her mouth was slippery and wet and hot with greedy want as it fed off his.

His hands moved from cupping her face to pressing against the small of her back, bringing her hard against him. Emelia felt the outline of his erection; it stirred something deep and primal in her. Her thighs trembled as she felt the slickness of need anointing her. She sent her hands on their own journey of discovery: the hard planes of his back and shoulders, the taut trimness of his waist, the leanness of his hips and the heat and throbbing of his blood rising so proud and insistent from between his legs.

He groaned against her mouth, something unintelligible, a mixture of Spanish, English and desperation as her fingers freed him from his clothing. He stepped out of the pool of his trousers, his shoes thudding to the floor as he succumbed to her touch. She felt another punch of lust in her belly. She wondered if this was how it had been from the start of their relationship. Physical attraction that was unstoppable, not underpinned with feelings other than primal lust.

Javier shrugged himself out of his shirt, tossing it aside before he started to work on hers. He pulled her top away from one of her shoulders, his hot mouth caressing the smooth flesh he had uncovered. Emelia gave herself up to the heady feel of his lips and teeth, her legs quivering with expectation as he continued the sensual journey, removing her clothes and replacing them with his mouth until she was standing in nothing but her lacy knickers.

His eyes were almost completely black as he stood looking at her, his hands on her hips, his touch sending livewires of need to her core.

Emelia's fingers splayed over his chest, the hard smooth muscles delighting her, the thunder of his heartbeat against her palm. She pressed a hot wet kiss to his throat, moving down, through the rough dark hair that narrowed from his chest to his groin. She went to her knees in front of him and he sprang up against her, hard, hot and swollen. She breathed over him, the air from her mouth making him tense all over. She touched him with the tip of her tongue, a light experimental taste that had him gripping her by the shoulders, his fingers digging in almost painfully as he anchored himself. She stroked her tongue along the satin length of him, feeling each pulsing ridge of his flesh, delighting in the way his breathing intervals shortened, the way the muscles of his abdomen clenched and his fingers dug even deeper into the flesh of her shoulders.

Before she could complete her sensual mission he hauled her back up to her feet, his eyes almost feverish with desire as they locked on hers. 'Enough of that for now,' he said. 'I won't last.'

Emelia could feel the pressure building inside him and wanted to feel it inside her, to feel him stretching her, filling her, possessing her totally, irrevocably.

His mouth came back to hers, hungrily, feeding off her with a new desperation as his body pulsed with urgency against hers. His hand cupped her feminine mound, a possessive touch that made every hair on her scalp lift in anticipation. The lacy barrier of her knickers only intensified the scalding heat of his touch. She arched up against him, an unspoken need crying out from every pore of her flesh.

He moved her to the bed, guiding her, pushing her, urging her with his mouth still seared to hers, his tongue enslaving hers.

Emelia gasped as he peeled her knickers away, the brush of lace against her thighs nothing to what it felt like to have his mouth do the same. His hot breath whispered down her thighs and up again and then against her feminine folds, his fingers gently separating her, his tongue tasting her like an exotic elixir. She whimpered as the sensations rippled through her, everything in her fizzled and sparked with feeling. She writhed under his erotic touch, panting against the building crescendo. Her fingers dug into the cover on the bed, her heart racing as he continued his shockingly intimate caress until she finally exploded. It was a hundred sensations at once: a cataclysmic eruption, a tidal wave, a landslide, every nerve twitching in the aftermath, her chest rising and falling as her breathing fought to return to normal. She felt limbless, floating on a cloud of release, wondering how many times he had done this to her. How could she have forgotten such rapture?

But it was not over.

Javier moved up over her, his strong thighs gently nudging hers apart, his erection brushing against her swollen flesh. His expression was contorted with concentration, a fierce determination to keep control. She felt it in the way he held himself as if he was worried he would hurt her in his own quest for release. She reassured him by stroking his back, urging him to complete the union, positioning her body to receive him, aching to feel that musky male thickness inside her.

He groaned as he surged into her slick warmth, the skin of his back lifting under her fingertips. She felt him check himself but she was having none of it. She urged him on again, lifting her hips to meet the downward thrust of his, the pumping action of his body sending waves of shivering delight through her. His breathing quickened, his body rocking with increasing speed, carrying her along with him on the racing breakneck tide. She felt the stabbing heat of him, the primal rush of her senses pulling her into another vortex. She arched some more, the tight ache beginning all over again as he thrust all the harder and faster. She panted beneath the sweat-slicked heat of him, the hairs on his chest tickling her breasts, her molten core tingling for that final trigger that would send her to paradise once more.

He slid one of his hands down between their rocking

bodies, his fingers finding the swollen-with-need pearl of her body, the stroking motion tipping her over the edge into oblivion.

As she was swirling back from the abyss of pleasure she felt him work himself to orgasm, the way he thrust on, his breathing ragged and heavy, his primal-sounding grunts as he finally let go making her shiver all over in response.

The silence was heavy and scented with sex.

Emelia opened her eyes after timeless minutes to see Javier propped up on his elbows, looking down at her with those unreadable black eyes. She felt shy all of a sudden. She had not thought her body capable of such feeling, of such powerful mind-blowing responses. He had stirred her so deeply, and not just physically. It was more than that, so much more. She felt a feather brush over her heart. She felt a fluttering feeling in her stomach, like the wings of a small bird. She tried to hold on to the image that had appeared like a ghost inside her mind, but it vaporised into nothingness before she could make sense of it.

Javier brushed a damp strand of her hair back from her face. 'You have a faraway look on your face,' he said.

Emelia blinked herself back to the present. 'I thought I remembered something else but it's gone.'

As if sensing her frustration, he bent his head and kissed her forehead softly. 'As long as you don't forget this,' he said, kissing both of her eyebrows in turn. 'And this.' He kissed the end of her nose. 'And this.' He kissed the corner of her mouth and she turned her head so her lips met his.

The heat leapt from his mouth to hers, the lightning

flash of his tongue meeting hers causing an instant con-
flagration of the senses. Emelia felt the stiffening of his
body where it was still encased in hers, the rapid rise
of her pulse in time with his as he started moving within
her. She ran her fingers through his hair, down over his
shoulders, his back and then grasped the firm flesh of
his buttocks, relishing the tension she could feel
building in his body.

'It is always this way between us,' he growled against
her mouth. 'Once is never enough. I want you like I
want no other woman. This need, it never goes away.'

Emelia felt a spurt of feminine pride that she had
captivated his desire in such a way. 'I want you too,' she
said, giving herself up to his passionately determined
kiss.

He left her mouth to suckle on her breasts, a light
teasing movement of his lips that left her breathless for
more. He kissed the sensitive underside of each breast
before coming back to her mouth, crushing it beneath
his as his need for release built.

This time his lovemaking was fast and furious, as if
all the frustration at her not remembering could only be
expressed through the passionate connection of their
bodies. He rolled her over until she was on top, his
hands cupping her breasts as his dark eyes held hers.
'You like it like this, *querida*,' he said in a deep gravelly
voice. 'Make yourself come against me. Let me watch
you.'

Shyness gripped her but the sensual challenge was
too tempting to ignore. She could feel him against her
most sensitive point when she shifted slightly. It was
like a match to a flame to feel him hard and thick against
her, the friction so delicious she was gasping out loud

as she rode him unashamedly. She came apart within seconds, her cries of ecstasy ringing in the silence, her breathing choppy and her heart rate uneven.

He used her last few contractions to bring himself to completion, his eyes now screwed shut, his face contorted with the exquisite pleasure he was feeling. Emelia felt him empty himself, each rocking pulse of his body triggering aftershocks in hers.

She slumped down over him, more out of shyness than exhaustion, although her limbs felt leaden after so much pleasure. She felt his fingers absently stroking over each knob of her spine, lingering over her lower vertebrae, his touch still lighting fires beneath her skin.

When he spoke his voice reverberated against her chest. 'Did that trigger anything in your memory?'

Emelia opened her eyes and, raising her head, looked down at him. Her heart squeezed in her chest as if a hand were closing into a fist around it. His dark eyes were like liquid, melted by passion, warm and softer than she had ever seen them. A feeling rushed up from deep inside her, an overwhelming sense of rightness. It was like a door creaking open in her head. Memories started filing through, like soldiers called to action. It was blurry at first, but then it cleared as she put the pieces together in her mind.

She remembered their first meeting. She remembered the way he had met her gaze across the room and how her fingers had stumbled on the piece she was playing. She had quickly looked away, embarrassed, feeling gauche and unsophisticated as she continued playing through her repertoire. She had never before reacted like that to any man who had come in. It had been an almost visceral thing. His presence seemed to reach out across the space that divided them and touch her.

She remembered how he had come over to the piano when she was packing up and asked her to join him for a drink. An hour later he had offered to drive her home, an offer she politely declined. He came the next night and the next, sitting listening to her play, slowly sipping at his drink, watching her until she finished. And each night he would offer to drive her home. By the third night she agreed. She remembered how she fell in love with him after their first kiss. She remembered how it felt to feel his arms go around her and draw her close to his body, the way her body felt in response, the way her heart beat until it felt as if it was going to work its way out of her chest.

She remembered the first time they made love. It was a month after they had met. He had been so gentle and patient, schooling her into the delights of her own body and the heat and potency of his. She could feel herself blushing just thinking about where they had gone from there. How eager she had been to learn, how willing she had been to be everything he wanted in a partner and then as his wife.

In spite of her initial reservations, she had moulded herself into the role, trying so hard to fit into his life-style, fashioning herself into the sort of trophy wife she assumed he wanted: a rail-thin clothes horse, a glamour girl always with a glass of champagne in one hand and a brilliant smile pasted on her perfectly made-up face. She had ignored the doubts that kept lurking in the shadows of her mind. Doubts about the way he refused to discuss his feelings, doubts about his adamantine stance about not having children, doubts about having signed the prenuptial document he'd insisted she sign, doubts about the intimidation she felt when alone at the villa with just his staff for company when he was away on business, which he seemed to be so often.

She had begun to feel she didn't really belong in his life and that the fiery attraction that had brought them together initially was not going to be enough to sustain them in the long term. She had always known he desired her; it was the one thing she could count on. He never seemed to tire of making love with her. It had thrilled her at first but after a while she had begun to crave more from him than sex. She had fooled herself she would be able to change him, to teach him how to love her the way she loved him.

And then, in spite of what she had told him, she had begun to dream of having a baby. She silently craved to build a family with him, to put down the roots that had been denied her throughout her childhood. But she had never been brave enough to bring up the subject. She had obediently taken her contraceptive pills and done her best to ignore the screeching clamour of her biological clock until that fateful day when she had finally had enough. Finding out about his father's will, on top of the press photo of him with the Russian singer, had tipped her over the edge. She had left him in the hope he would come after her and beg her to return. She had hoped he would insist on changing the rules of their marriage so they could have a proper fulfilling life together.

But of course he hadn't. A man as proud as Javier would not beg anyone to come back to him. Look at what had happened between him and his father. A decade had gone past and he hadn't budged.

'Emelia?' Javier's deep voice broke through her thoughts. 'What's going on?'

She met his concerned gaze. 'I remember…'

He sat upright, tumbling her onto her back, his fingers grasping her by both arms. 'What? Everything?' he asked.

She shook her head. 'Bits and pieces. Like when and how we met. Some of our time together. Most of our time together.'

One of his hands moved in a slow stroking motion up and down her arm. 'So I was right,' he said. 'Your body recognised me from the first. Your mind just had to catch up.'

She touched his lips with her fingers, tracing over their contours. 'How could I have forgotten you? I can't believe I didn't remember you. Were you very angry about that?'

Javier captured one of her fingers with his mouth, sucking on it erotically, all the while holding her gaze. He released her finger and said, 'I have to admit I was angry, especially when you hadn't forgotten Marshall.'

Her eyes dropped from his, a frown pulling at her forehead. 'I can't explain that. I'm sorry.'

'It is not important now,' he said. 'We have to move on.'

'Javier?' Her soft voice was like a feather brushing along his lower spine.

Javier looked down at her tussled hair and slim naked body. His groin tightened as he thought of having her back in his life permanently. His plans to divorce her seemed so ridiculous now. He had acted stupidly, blindly and in anger. His pride had taken a hit from what had been reported in the press about her and Marshall and he had let it block out his reason. He wanted her too much to let her go. He didn't like admitting it. He would rather die than admit it. She was the one woman who had brought him to his knees. He had nearly gone out of his head when he found she had left him. He had not realised how much he wanted and needed her until she had gone.

A part of him blamed himself. He had been so pre-occupied with the Moscow takeover. It was the deal of a lifetime. The negotiations had been tricky from the get-go but he had always believed he could pull it off. His goal had been to add that Russian bank to his empire and he had done it. It was the ultimate prize, the bench-mark business deal. But he just hadn't realised it would come at such a personal cost.

He brushed some damp tendrils of hair back off her face. 'Tired, *cariño*?'

She shook her head, her grey-blue eyes like shimmering pools. 'Not at all.' She stretched her slim body against him just like a sinuous cat and smiled. 'Not one little bit.'

His blood rocketed through his veins and he pressed her back down and covered her mouth with his, kissing her hungrily, delighting in the way she responded just as greedily. His tongue played with hers, stroking and sweeping until she succumbed with a whimpering sigh of pleasure. His hands moved over her breasts, the already erect nipples a dark cherry-red. He closed his mouth over each of them, flicking them with the point of his tongue, before sucking deeply. Her fingers scored through his hair, her body bucking under him as she opened for him.

He knew he was rushing things but he was aching

and heavy with longing. She was already slick with his seed from before, hot, wet and wanting him just as much as he wanted her. It sounded prehistoric but he wanted to stake his claim again and again, to mark his territory in the most primal way of all. Her body wrapped around him tightly as he thrust into her, the walls of her inner core rippling against him. He had to fight to stay in control, each thrusting movement sending gushing waves of need right through him. She squirmed beneath him, searching for that extra friction to send her to paradise. He made her wait; he wanted to make her beg. It seemed fitting since he had suffered so much because of her leaving him, for putting him through such a tormented hell.

'I want…' she panted beneath him. 'I want you to… Oh, please, Javier…'

He smiled over her mouth as he took it in another scorching kiss, his hands sliding between her thighs, teasing her with almost-there caresses.

She whimpered again and grasped at his hand, pushing it against her pearly need. 'Please,' she begged him passionately.

Javier flicked his fingers against her, just the way she liked. He knew her body like a maestro knew his instrument. She felt so silky and feminine, the scent of her driving him mad with the need to let go. He waited until she had started to orgasm, the spasms of her body gripping him until he had no choice but to explode. He pumped into her harder and harder, forcing the images of her alleged affair that had tortured him out of his head. He felt her flinch, he even felt her fingers grasping at his shoulders but he carried on relentlessly, until finally he spilled himself with a shout of triumph.

He rolled onto his back, his chest rising and falling as he tried to steady his breathing. He turned his head as he felt the mattress shift. Emelia had rolled away with her back to him, huddled into a ball. He reached out and stroked a finger down her spine. 'Emelia?'

She flinched and moved further away from him, mumbling something he didn't quite catch.

Javier sat upright and, taking her nearest shoulder, turned her onto her back. 'What's wrong?' he asked.

Her eyes flashed at him like lightning. 'I think you know what's wrong.'

'I'm not a mind reader, Emelia. If you have something to say, then, for God's sake, say it.'

She continued to glare at him but then her eyes began to swim with tears. 'Don't ever make love to me as if I was your mistress,' she said, her voice cracking over the words. 'I am your wife.'

Javier felt a knife of guilt go between his ribs. 'I got carried away,' he said. 'I'm sorry. You said you liked it like that in the past.'

She gave him a cutting look. 'Did you ever think I might have been saying that just to please you?'

He sent his fingers through his hair before he reluctantly faced her. 'I am not sure of what you want any more, Emelia,' he said. 'It's like I have a different wife from the one I had only a month or so ago. It's going to take some time to adjust.'

She looked at him through watery eyes. 'Was our relationship about anything but sex?' she asked.

He got off the bed as if she had pushed him. 'Now that some of your memory has returned you should know how much I detest these sorts of discussions,' he said with a harsh note of annoyance. 'I laid out the terms of our marriage and you agreed to them. Now you want to change things.'

She pulled the bedcovers over her. 'Why don't you just answer the question? Did you ever feel anything for me other than desire? Did you love me, even just a little?'

Javier tried to stare her down but she held firm. He let out a savage breath. 'My father told me he loved me but it didn't mean a thing. It was conditional, if anything. He wanted me to be a puppet. As soon as I wanted to choose my own path, his love was cut off.'

'That was wrong of him,' she said. 'Parents should never withhold their love, not for any reason.'

He made a scoffing sound in his throat. 'My father loved his wives, all four of them, and they apparently loved him back, but look where that ended—an early death and two, almost three, very expensive divorces.'

Her brow wrinkled with a frown. 'So what you're saying is you don't believe love can ever last?'

'It's not a reliable emotion, Emelia. It changes all the time.'

'I'm not sure what you're saying in relation to us…'

'The things that make a relationship work are common ground and chemistry,' Javier said. 'A bit of mutual respect doesn't go amiss either.'

Her expression was crestfallen and he felt every kind of heel as a result. Was he incapable of loving or just resistant to being that vulnerable to another person? He couldn't answer with any certainty.

'Don't push me on this, Emelia,' he said into the silence. 'Our relationship has been through so much of late. This is not the time to be saying things neither of us are certain is true.'

'But I know I love you,' she said. 'I know it with absolute certainty. I loved you from the first moment I met you. I didn't tell you because I knew you didn't want to hear it. But I need to tell you now. I can't hold it in any longer.'

He pinned her with his gaze. 'You speak of loving me and yet you were leaving me, Emelia, or have you not remembered that part? You had given up on our relationship. You wouldn't be here now if you hadn't been injured and lost your memory. You would be back in Australia. You were in that car with Marshall because he was driving you to the airport.'

Her teeth sank into her bottom lip until it went white.

'Why don't we wait until all the pieces are in place before you start planning the future?' he said when she didn't speak. 'Unless we deal with the past, we might not even have a future.'

'You…you want a divorce?' Her voice sounded like a wounded child's.

'I don't believe we should stay shackled together if one or both of us is unhappy,' he said. 'We'll give it a month or two and reassess. It is early days. You've only just come out of hospital after a near-fatal accident. You're damned lucky to be alive.'

Her mouth went into a pout. 'No doubt it would have been much better for you if I had been killed.'

Javier ground his teeth as he thought about that moment when Aldana had informed him there was a call from the police in London. His heart had nearly stopped until he had been assured she hadn't been fatally wounded. 'My mother died when she was three years younger than you are,' he said. 'She didn't see my first day at school. She didn't hear the first words I learned to read. I didn't get the chance to tell her how much I loved her or if I did I was too young to remember doing it. Don't you dare tell me I would rather have you dead and buried. No one deserves to have their life cut short through the stupidity of other's actions.'

She sent him a defiant glare. 'Maybe it suits you to have me alive so you can pay me back for daring to leave you. I bet I'm the first woman who ever has.'

Javier drew in a sharp breath. 'You're the one who moved the goalposts, not me.'

'I can't be the sort of wife you want,' she said, her eyes shining with tears. 'I can't do it any more. I'm not that sort of person, Javier. I want more from life than money and sex and endless hours in the gym or the beauty salon. I want to be loved for who I am, not for what I look like.'

He snatched up his trousers and zipped himself into them. 'I care about you, Emelia. Believe me, you would not be here now if I didn't.'

'Is that supposed to make me feel better?' she asked. 'You *care* about me. For God's sake, Javier, you make me sound like some sort of pet.'

He sent her a frustrated look as he grasped the door handle. 'We will talk about this later,' he said. 'You are not yourself right now.'

'You're damn right I'm not,' she said. 'But that's the heart of the problem. I have never been myself the whole time we've been married. I am a fake wife, Javier, a complete and utter fraud. How long do you expect such a marriage to last?'

He set his mouth. 'It will last until I say it's over.' And then he opened the door and strode out, snapping the door shut behind him.

CHAPTER EIGHT

EMELIA went to bed totally wrung out after her conversation with Javier. She lay awake for hours, hoping he might come in and join her but he apparently wanted to keep his distance. She spent a restless night, agonising over everything, ruminating over all the stupid decisions she had made, all the crazy choices to be with him in spite of how little he was capable of giving her emotionally. No wonder she had grown tired of their arrangement. She was amazed it had lasted as long as it had. She had compromised herself in every way possible. With the wisdom of hindsight, she knew that if she'd had better self-esteem she would never have agreed to such a marriage. But, plagued with insecurities stemming from childhood, she had been knocked off her feet with his passionate attention. His ruthless determination to have her in his bed had curdled her common sense. She had acted on impulse, not sensibly.

When she woke the next morning after snatches of troubled sleep she felt the beginnings of a vicious headache. The light spilling in from the gap in the curtains was like steel skewers driving through her skull. She groaned and buried her head under the pillow, nausea rolling in her stomach like an out of control boulder.

The sound of the door opening set a shockwave of pain through her head and she groaned again, but this time it came out more like a whimper.

'*Mi amor?*' Javier strode quickly towards the bed. 'Are you unwell?'

Emelia slowly turned her head to face him, her eyes half-open. 'I have the most awful headache…'

He placed a cool dry hand on her forehead, making her want to cry like a small child at the tender gesture. 'You're hot but I don't think you're feverish,' he said. 'I'll check your temperature and then call for the doctor.'

Right at that moment Emelia didn't care if he called for the undertaker. She was consumed with the relentless, torturous pain. The nausea intensified and, before he could come back with a thermometer, she stumbled into the en suite bathroom and dispensed with the meagre contents of her stomach in wretched heaves that burned her throat.

Javier came in behind her. 'Ah, *querida*,' he said soothingly. 'Poor baby. You really are sick.' He dampened a face cloth and gently lifted her hair off the back of her neck and pressed the coolness of the cloth there.

Emelia brushed her teeth once the nausea had abated. She slowly turned, embarrassed at her loss of dignity. She felt so weak and being in Javier's strong, commanding presence only seemed to intensify her feelings of feeble vulnerability. She could not remember a time when she had been sick in front of him before. He was always so robustly healthy and energetic, which had made her feel as if he would be revolted by any sign of weakness or fragility. In the past she had hidden any of her various and mostly minor ailments, putting on a brave face and carrying on her role of the always perfect, always biddable wife.

'The doctor is on her way,' he said, supporting her by the elbow. 'Why don't you get back into bed and close your eyes for a bit?'

'I'm sorry about this…' she said once she was back in bed. 'I thought I was getting better.'

'I am sure you are but perhaps yesterday was too much for you,' he said. He brushed the hair back from her face, his expression more than a little rueful. 'I'm sorry for upsetting you. I keep forgetting you're not well enough to go head to head with me.'

'I am fine…really…'

He grimaced and added, 'I shouldn't have made love with you. Perhaps it was too soon.'

Emelia wasn't sure what to say so stayed silent. It seemed safer than admitting how much she had wanted him to make love to her.

There was the sound of someone arriving downstairs and Javier rose from the bed. 'That sounds like the doctor,' he said. 'I'll be right back.'

Within a couple of minutes a female doctor came in, who had clearly been briefed by Javier, and she briskly introduced herself and proceeded to examine Emelia, checking both of her pupils along with her blood pressure.

'Have you had migraines in the past?' Eva Garcia asked as she put the portable blood pressure machine back in her bag before taking out a painkiller vial and needle for injection.

'Not that I can remember,' Emelia said. 'But I've had a few headaches since I had the accident a couple of weeks ago.'

'Your husband tells me you've recovered a bit of your memory,' Eva said, preparing Emelia's arm for the injection. 'That was yesterday, correct?'

'Yes…'

'You need to take things more slowly,' Dr Garcia said. 'I'm going to take some bloods just to make sure there's nothing else going on.'

Emelia felt a hand of panic clutch at her throat, imagining an intracranial haemorrhage or the onset of a stroke from a clot breaking loose. 'What else could be going on?' she asked hollowly.

The doctor took out a tourniquet and syringe set. 'You could be low on iron or have some underlying issue to do with your head injury.' She expertly took the blood and pressed down on the puncture site, her eyes meeting Emelia's. 'What about your periods? Are they regular?'

Emelia was suddenly glad Javier had left the room as soon as he had brought the doctor in. 'Um…I really can't remember…'

'So you haven't had one since the accident?'

Emelia bit her lip. 'No…'

'Don't worry,' the doctor said. 'After the ordeal you've been through, your system is probably going to take some time to settle down. Stress, trauma, especially physical as in your case, would be enough to temporarily shut down the menstrual cycle. Are you taking any form of oral contraception?'

'My prescription has run out,' Emelia said. 'I wasn't sure whether to go back on it or not. I thought I should wait until…until I knew more about…things…'

'I'll write you one up, just in case.' The doctor took out her prescription pad and Emelia told her the brand name and dose.

Within another minute or two the doctor was being seen out and Javier came back in. 'How are you feeling now? Headache still bad?'

'The doctor gave me an injection,' she said. 'It's starting to work. I'm already feeling a bit sleepy.'

He stroked a hand over her forehead. 'I'll bring something for you to drink. Do you fancy anything to eat?'

Emelia winced at the thought of food. 'No. Please, no food.'

His hand lingered for a moment on her cheek before he left her, closing the door so softly Emelia hardly heard it as her eyelids fluttered down over her eyes...

When she woke it was well into the evening. She gingerly got out of bed and dragged herself into the shower. As she came out of the bathroom, wrapped in nothing but a towel, the bedroom door opened and Javier came in.

'Feeling better?' he asked.

'A lot.' Emelia tried to smile but it didn't quite work. 'Thank you.'

'Do you feel up to having some dinner?' he asked. 'Aldana's prepared something for us.'

'I'll just get dressed,' she said, feeling shy, as if she was on her first date with him.

She could see he was trying hard to put her at ease. He had been so gentle earlier, so concerned for her welfare she wondered if he loved her just a tiny bit after all. She chided herself for dreaming of what he couldn't or wouldn't give. As much as she loved him, she couldn't afford to waste any more of her life waiting for him to change. If he didn't want the same things in life she did, then she would have to have the courage to move on without him, for his sake as well as her own. She hated to think of never seeing his face again or, worse, imagining him with some other woman. How would she endure it?

'Take your time,' he said, gently flicking her cheek with the end of his finger. 'I have some business proposals to read through.'

She touched her face when he left, wishing for the moon that was so far out of reach it was heartbreaking.

Javier came back to find Emelia dressed in a simple black dress that skimmed her slim form, highlighting the gentle swell of her breasts and the long trim legs encased—unusually for her—in ballet flats. Her hair had been blow-dried but, rather than styling it, she had pulled it back into a simple ponytail. She had the barest minimum of make-up on, just a brush of mascara which intensified the grey-blue of her eyes, and a pink shade of lip gloss which drew attention to her soft full mouth with its rounded upper lip. He felt the heat of arousal surge into his groin as he remembered how that mouth felt around him. She was the most naturally sensual woman he had ever met and yet at times, especially right now, he seriously wondered if she was aware of it.

'You are looking very beautiful this evening, *querida*,' he said.

She smoothed her hands down over the flatness of her stomach as if she was conscious of the close-fitting nature of the dress. 'Thank you,' she murmured and shifted her gaze from his to pick up a light wrap she had laid on the end of the bed.

He escorted her down the stairs, holding her hand in his, noting how her fingers trembled slightly as they approached the formal dining room.

Aldana brought in the meal and Javier watched as Emelia kept her gaze down, as if she was frightened of saying or doing the wrong thing. He was the first to recognise that Aldana was a difficult person, but she was dependent on the income he gave her after her husband had gambled away everything they had owned. Javier didn't want to dispense with her services just because of a personality clash with his wife, but he could see Emelia was on edge and he had cause to wonder if things were worse when he wasn't around to keep an eye on things.

After watching Emelia pick at her food for several minutes, he dabbed his napkin at the edges of his mouth and laid it back over his lap. 'Emelia,' he said, 'I know, like many women, you are keen to keep slim, but I have never agreed with you starving yourself. In my opinion, you were perfectly fine the way you were when I first met you. There is no need to deny yourself what you want. Your health is much more important.'

She looked up at him with a sheepish expression. 'I haven't been to the gym once since I've been home. I can't believe I did it before. Izabella said I was obsessive about it. I normally have no self-discipline. I much prefer incidental exercise, like walking or swimming.'

'And sex?' he asked with a teasing smile.

Her face coloured and she lowered her gaze to her plate. 'Is that all you think about?' she asked in a tight little voice.

'It's what we both used to think about,' he said. 'You are the most sensually aware woman I have ever been with.'

Her grey-blue eyes flashed back to his. 'And I bet there have been hundreds.'

He took a moment to respond. 'You knew about my lifestyle when we met. I have made it no secret that I lived a fast-paced life.'

'Which is no doubt why you wanted a shallow smokescreen marriage to impress your business contacts,' she put in. 'I can't believe I agreed to it. I never wanted to turn out like my poor mother, preening herself constantly in case her wayward husband strayed to someone slimmer or better looking or better groomed or better dressed.'

Javier frowned at the sudden vehemence of her words. Her face was pinched and her mouth tight and her shoulders tense. Without her veneer of sophistication, she looked young and vulnerable, and yet she looked far more beautiful than he had ever seen her. 'I didn't realise you felt like that,' he said after a little pause. 'You always seemed so confident. I didn't know you felt so unsure of yourself.'

Her throat moved up and down, as if she regretted revealing her insecurities to him. 'I haven't been honest with you,' she said. 'I mean right from the start. I should have told you but I was frightened you would walk away, that I would appear too needy or something. I guess back then I wanted you on any terms. I was prepared to suspend everything I wanted in life to be with you.'

He reached out a hand and picked up one of hers, entwining his fingers with her soft trembling ones. 'I don't want to lose you, *querida*,' he said. 'But I can only give you what I can give you. It might not be enough.'

She pressed her lips together, he assumed to stop herself from crying, but even so her eyes moistened. 'I want to be loved, Javier,' she said softly. 'I want to be loved the way my mother craved to be loved but never got to be loved. I want to wake up each morning knowing the man I love is right there by my side, supporting me, loving me, cherishing me.' She drew in an uneven breath and added in an even softer voice, 'And I want a baby.'

Javier felt a shockwave go through his chest. He recalled his lonely childhood: the ache of sudden loss, the devastation of being cast aside by his father after his mother had died. He could not face the responsibility of being a parent. He would mess it up, for sure. Even people from secure backgrounds occasionally ran into trouble with their kids. What chance would *he* have? He would end up ruining a child's potential, crippling them emotionally, stunting their development or making them hate him as much as he had ended up hating his own father for his inadequacies.

He couldn't risk it.

He *would not* risk it.

'That is not negotiable,' he found himself saying in a cold hard voice that he could scarcely believe was coming from his throat. 'There is no way I want children. I told you that right from the start and you were in total agreement.'

She looked at him with anguished eyes that scored his soul. 'I only accepted those terms because I was blindsided by love. I still love you, Javier, more than ever, but I don't want to miss out on having children.'

Javier pushed out his chair and got to his feet. 'You can't spring this sort of stuff on me, Emelia,' he said. 'Less than a month ago everything was fine between us. It was fine for almost two years. You did your thing. I did mine.' He pointed his finger at her. 'You are the one who suddenly changed things.'

Emelia put up her chin. 'I'm tired of doing things your way. I'm tired of seeing your picture splashed over every international paper with yet another wannabe model or starlet. Surely you have more control over who you are seen with?'

He clamped down on his jaw. 'The person I should be seen with is my wife,' he said. 'But she is always too busy shopping in another country or having her hair or nails done.'

Emelia flinched at his stinging words. But perhaps the sliver of truth in them was what hurt the most. She had been caught up in the world of being his wife instead of being his companion and soulmate. There was a big difference and it was a shame it had taken this long for her to see it. 'I'm sorry,' she said. 'I thought I was doing what you wanted.'

There was a stiff silence.

'Forget I said that,' Javier said. 'I didn't exactly make it easy on you on the few occasions you came with me. I am perhaps too task-oriented. I tend to focus on the big picture and lose sight of the details.'

'We've both made mistakes,' she said. 'I guess we just have to try not to make them again.'

He pushed his hand through his hair. 'I want this to work, Emelia,' he said. 'I want us to be happy, like we were before.'

'Javier, you were happy but I wasn't, not really,' she

said. 'My accident has shown me what a lie I've been living. The woman you want in your life is not the one I am now. I have never been that person.'

He came over and took her hands in his, pulling her to her feet. 'You *were* happy, Emelia,' he said, squeezing her hands for effect. 'I gave you everything money could buy. You wanted for nothing. I made sure of it.'

Emelia tried to pull away but he held firm. 'You're not listening to me, Javier. We can't go back to what we were before. *I* can't go back.'

'Let's see about that, shall we?' he said and brought his mouth down hard on hers.

At first Emelia made a token resistance but her heart wasn't in it. She wanted him any way she could get him, even if it was in anger or to prove a point. At least he was showing some emotion, even if it was not the one she most wanted him to demonstrate. She kissed him back with the same heat and fire, her tongue tangling with his in a sensual battle of wills.

He pressed her back against the nearest wall, pulling down the zip at the back of her dress, letting it fall into a black puddle at her feet, his mouth still locked on hers. She clawed at his waistband, her fingers releasing his belt in a quest to uncover him.

He tore his mouth off hers. 'Not here,' he said. 'Aldana might come in to clear the table. Let's take this upstairs.'

Emelia had her chance then to call an end to this madness but still she let her heart rule her head. Later, she barely recalled how they got upstairs; she seemed to remember the journey was interspersed with hot drugging kisses that ramped up her need of him unbearably.

By the time they got to the bedroom she was almost delirious with desire. He came down heavily on top of her on the bed, his weight pinning her, his mouth crushing hers in a red-hot kiss that made her toes curl.

He removed her bra and cupped her breasts possessively, subjecting them to the fiery brand of his mouth. He went lower, over the plane of her belly, lingering over the dish of her belly button before he parted her thighs. She gulped in a breath as he stroked her with his tongue, the raw intimacy as he tasted her making her spine unhinge. She felt the tension building and building to snapping point, the waves of pleasure coming towards her from a distance and then suddenly they swamped her, tossing her around and around in a wild sea of sensual pleasure that superseded anything she had felt before.

Then he drove into her roughly at first and then checked himself, murmuring something that sounded like an apology before he continued in a rhythmic motion that triggered all of her senses into another climb to the summit of release. His thrusts came closer together, a little deeper each time, his breathing intervals shortening as he approached the ultimate moment.

Emelia felt her body preparing for another freefall into pleasure. She pushed her hips up to intensify the feeling his body provoked as it rubbed against her point of pleasure, her breathing becoming increasingly ragged as she felt the tremors begin. This time when her orgasm started she pushed against him as if trying to expel him from her body, the action triggering her G spot, sending her into an earth-shattering release that rippled through her for endless seconds.

Javier came with an explosive rush, his deep grunt

of ecstasy sending shivers of delight down Emelia's spine. This was the only time she felt he allowed himself to be vulnerable. She clung to him as he emptied himself, the shudders of his body as it pinned her to the bed reverberating through her. She kept her arms wrapped around him, hoping he wouldn't roll away and spoil the moment.

'Am I too heavy for you?' he asked against the soft skin of her neck.

'No,' she said as she ran her fingers up and down his back.

He lifted himself on his elbows, looking down at her for a lengthy moment. 'I didn't hurt you, did I?'

She shook her head. 'No.'

His eyes travelled to her mouth, watching as she moistened it with her tongue. 'Still unhappy?' he asked.

Emelia searched his features for any sign of mockery but she couldn't find anything to suggest he was taunting her. But then he was a master at inscrutability when he chose to be. Even his dark eyes gave nothing away. 'There are times when I am not sure what I feel,' she said, taking the middle ground.

His mouth tilted in a rueful smile. 'I suppose I deserve that.'

Emelia let a silence underline his almost apology.

After another moment or two he lifted himself off her, offering her a hand to get up. 'Want to have a shower with me?'

The invitation she could see in the dark glitter of his eyes stirred her senses into a heated frenzy. How could he do this to her so soon after such mind-blowing satiation? Just one look and he had her quivering with need all over again. Wordlessly, she took his hand, allowing him to lead her into the en suite bathroom, standing to one side as he turned on the shower lever that was set at a controlled temperature.

He stepped under the spray and pulled her in under it with him. The fine needles of hot water cascaded over them as he brought his mouth to hers. It was a softer kiss this time, a leisurely exploration of her mouth that lured her into a sensual whirlpool. His tongue swept over hers, stroking and gliding with growing urgency, his erection hot and heavy against her belly. She slid down the shower stall and took him in her hands, exploring him with sensuous movements that brought his breathing to a stumbling halt. 'Careful, *cariño*,' he said. 'I might not be able to hold back.'

'I don't care,' she said recklessly.

She gave him a sultry look from beneath her lashes before taking him in her mouth in one slick movement that provoked a rough expletive from him. She smiled around his throbbing heat, her tongue gliding wetly along his length. She tasted his essence, inciting her to draw more of him into her mouth. His hands shot out to the glass walls of the shower to anchor himself, his thighs set apart, his chest rising and falling as he struggled to control his breathing. 'You don't have to do this,' he said, but the subtext, she knew, was really: *please don't stop doing this*.

'I like doing this to you,' she said. 'You do it to me so it's only fair I get to do the same to you.'

He swallowed tightly, his jaw clenching as he watched her return to his swollen length. Emelia felt the tension in the satin-covered steel of his body. He was drawing closer and closer to the point of no return and it excited her to think she could have such a powerful hold over him.

He jerked and then shuddered into her mouth, spilling his hot life force, his flesh lifting in goose-bumps in spite of the warmth of the shower.

Emelia glided back up his body, rinsing her mouth under the shower spray before meeting his dark lustrous eyes. He didn't say anything. He just looked at her with dark intensity, his hands reaching for the soap and working up a lather. She quivered with anticipation as he started soaping her, firstly her neck and shoulders, and then her breasts, the length of her spine and then her belly. He used circular movements that set all her nerves into a frantic dance, his touch so smooth and sensual she felt every bone inside her frame melt.

His hand cupped her feminine mound, seeking the swollen nub of her desire. She felt her breathing come to a stumbling halt as he bent down before her as she had done to him. His tongue separated her, teasing her, a soft flicker at first and then increasing the pace until she was gasping her way through an orgasm that shook her like a rag doll.

She collapsed against him as he rose to hold her, his arms coming around her as she rested her head against his chest. His heart was drumming under her cheek, one of his hands coming up to stroke her wet hair. He rested his chin on the top of her head and for a moment she wondered if he was going to tell her he loved her after all, that he wanted the same things she wanted.

But of course he didn't. Instead, he turned off the water and silently reached for a bath towel, wrapping her in it as one would a small child.

Emelia stepped out of the shower cubicle and did her best to squash her disappointment. Was this intense physical attraction the only thing she could cling to in order to keep him by her side? How long would it last? What if he tired of her and went to someone else to fulfil his needs? The thought of it was like an arrow through her heart. She hated even thinking about all the partners he had had before her. He never spoke of them and she never asked, but she knew there had been many women who had come and gone from his bed.

Javier turned her face to look at him. 'What is that frown for?' he asked.

She gave him a half-smile. 'Nothing…I was just thinking.'

His hand moved to cradle her cheek. 'About what?'

She pressed her lips together momentarily. 'I don't know…just where this will lead, I guess.'

His hand dropped from her face. 'Life doesn't always fit into nice neat little boxes, Emelia,' he said. 'And it doesn't always give us everything we want.'

'What do you want from life?' she asked.

He paused in the process of drying himself to look at her. 'The same things most people want—success, a sense of purpose, fulfilment.'

'What about love?'

He tossed the damp towel on the bed. 'I don't delude myself that it's a given in life. Love comes and it goes. It's not something I have ever relied on.'

Emelia mentally kicked herself for setting herself up for more hurt. If he loved her, he would have told her by now. He'd had almost twenty-three months of marriage to do so, irrespective of what had occurred over the past couple of weeks.

'Come to bed, *querida*,' he said. 'You look like a child that has been kept up way past its bedtime.'

She crawled into bed, not for a moment thinking she

would be able to sleep after spending so much of the day in a drug-induced slumber, but somehow when Javier pulled her into his body she closed her eyes and, limb by limb, her body gradually relaxed until, with a soft sigh, she drifted off...

Javier lay with her in his arms, his fingers laced through the silky strands of her hair, breathing in its clean, newly washed fragrance. In sleep she looked so young and vulnerable. Her soft full mouth was slightly open and one of her hands was lying against his chest, right where his heart was beating.

He'd thought he had the future all mapped out but now he was not so sure. Things were changing almost daily. The more time he spent with her, the more he wanted to believe they could be in this for the long haul.

He tried to picture a child they might make together: a dark-haired little boy or perhaps a little girl with grey-blue eyes and hair just as silken and golden as her mother. But the image faded, as if there was no room in his head for it.

Perhaps it was fate. He wasn't meant to be a father. It wasn't that he didn't like children. One of his business colleagues had recently become a father and Javier had looked at the photos with a strange sense of loss. His lonely childhood had marked him for life. He couldn't imagine himself as a parent. He didn't think he would know what to do. He hated the thought of potentially damaging a child's self-esteem by saying or doing the wrong thing. Children seemed to him to be so vulnerable. *He* had been so vulnerable.

He had never forgotten the day his mother had died. She had been there one minute, soft and scented and nurturing, and the next her body was in a shiny black coffin covered with red roses. He still hated the sight of red roses, any roses, in fact. They made his stomach churn. Within a year he had been sent off to boarding school in England as his father couldn't handle his ongoing grief. Javier had taught himself not to love anything or anyone in case it was ripped away from him without warning.

The thing that worried him the most was that it might be too late to change.

CHAPTER NINE

EMELIA woke up in bed alone and when she came downstairs Aldana informed her that Javier had left to see to some business in Malaga and would be back later that evening. She handed her a note with pursed lips. Emelia thanked her politely and, taking a cup of tea with her, went out to the sunny terrace overlooking the gardens.

The note was simple and written in Javier's distinctive handwriting, the strong dark strokes reminding her of his aura of command and control. It read:

Didn't want to wake you. See you tonight. J.

Emelia felt disappointed she hadn't woken before he'd left. There was so much she still wanted to say to him. She felt he had sideswiped her yet again by enslaving her senses. It was always the way he dealt with conflict, by reminding her of how much she needed him. It made her less and less confident of him shifting to accommodate her needs. He still had control, as he had always done. Nothing had changed, except the depth to which she could be hurt all over again.

The phone rang a little later in the morning and Aldana came out to the pool where Emelia was doing some laps and handed her the cordless receiver. 'It is the doctor,' she said, leaving the receiver on the table next to the sun lounger.

Emelia got out of the pool and quickly dried her hands on her towel before she picked up the phone. 'Hello? This is Emelia Mélendez speaking.'

'Señora Mélendez, I have some results for you from the blood tests I took,' Eva Garcia said.

Emelia felt her stomach shuffle like the rapidly thumbed pages of a book. 'Y-yes?'

'You are pregnant.'

Emelia's fingers clenched the phone in her hand until her knuckles became white, her heart thumping like a swinging hammer against her breastbone. 'I...I am?'

'Yes,' Dr Garcia said. 'Of course I am not sure how far along. It can't be too many weeks, otherwise I am sure the doctors who examined you after your accident would have noticed. You had an abdominal CT scan at some stage, didn't you?'

'Yes,' she said, still reeling from the shock announcement. 'It was done to check for internal bleeding but it was all clear. But how can I be pregnant? I was taking the Pill, or at least I assume I was. I don't really remember that clearly.'

'Perhaps you missed a dose here and there,' Dr Garcia suggested. 'It is very easy to forget and with these low dose brands it can create a small window of fertility. If you can remember when your last menstrual period was, I can calculate how far along you might be.'

Emelia thought for a moment. 'I think it might have been about three or four weeks before the accident. I remember I got a stomach virus right after. I couldn't keep anything down for forty-eight hours.'

'That would have been enough to render the Pill ineffective,' Dr Garcia said. 'But if, as you say, your last period was well over a month ago, you had probably fallen pregnant before you went to London. It is still very early days, but that doesn't mean you are not having all the symptoms. Some women are more sensitive to the hormonal changes than others.'

Emelia wondered how much her headaches and nausea were the result of the accident or of the early stages of pregnancy. She wondered too if her decision to leave Javier had been an irrational one brought on by the surge of hormones in her body. She could recall being more emotional than usual, her frustration at his absence escalating to blowout point when he'd come back just as the newspaper article had appeared, showing him with the nightclub singer. She was almost thankful she couldn't remember that 'ugly scene' as he called it. She was almost certain she would have been as wanton and needy as ever. It would not have helped her cause, saying with one breath she wanted out and begging him to pleasure her with the next.

'Well, then,' the doctor continued in a businesslike manner, 'I'd like you to start some pregnancy vitamins and we can make an appointment now if you like so we can organise that ultrasound.'

Emelia ended the call a minute or two later, her head spinning so much she had to sit down on the sun lounger.

Pregnant.

She placed a hand on her smooth flat abdomen. It

seemed impossible to think a tiny life was growing inside there. What would Javier say? she wondered sickly. Would he think she had 'accidentally' fallen pregnant? He was so cynical, she couldn't see how else he would react. But she didn't for a moment believe she had done it on purpose. Yes, she had become increasingly unhappy about taking the Pill, but she would not have deliberately missed a dose. She had wanted Javier to commit to bringing a child into their relationship. Foisting one on him was not something she had thought fair. It was a joint decision that she had longed he would one day be ready to make, but now it seemed neither of them had made the decision—fate, chance or destiny had made it for them.

She spent the rest of the day in an emotional turmoil as she prepared herself for facing Javier. She would have to tell him. She couldn't possibly keep it from him. He had a right to know he was to become a father, even if it was the last thing he wanted to be.

She heard him arrive at eight in the evening. Each of his footfalls felt like hammer blows to her heart as he made his way into *la sala* where she was waiting. She stood as he came in, her hands in a tight knot in front of her stomach.

'Sorry I'm late,' he said, coming over to her. He brushed his knuckles down the curve of her cheek. 'You look pale, *querida*. You haven't been overdoing it, I hope.'

She gave him a nervous movement of her lips that sufficed for a smile. 'No, I spent most of the day by the pool. It was hot again today.'

He pressed a soft kiss to her bare shoulder. 'Mmm, you are a little pink here and there.' He met her eyes again. 'You shouldn't lie out there without protection. Did you put on sunscreen?'

Emelia lowered her gaze from his. 'I did have some on but it must have worn off while I was in the water.'

He tipped up her face, studying her with increasing intensity. 'Is something wrong?' he asked. 'You seem a little on edge.'

She took a breath but it caught on something in her chest. 'Javier…I have something to tell you…'

A frown pulled at his brow. 'You've remembered something else?'

She bit the inside of her mouth. 'No, it's not that. I…I got a call from the doctor.'

His eyes narrowed slightly and his voice sounded strangely hollow. 'There's nothing seriously wrong, is there?'

Emelia gave him a strained look. 'I guess it depends on how you look at it.'

'Whatever it is, we will deal with it,' he said. 'We'll get the best doctors and specialists. They can do just about anything these days with conditions that had no cure in the past.'

She couldn't quite remove the wryness from her tone. 'This isn't a condition you can exactly cure, or at least not for a few months.'

'Are you going to tell me or am I supposed to guess?' he asked after a slight pause.

Emelia could feel his suspicion growing. She could see it in his dark eyes, the way they had narrowed even further, his frown deepening. She took another uneven breath. 'Javier, I'm pregnant.'

The words fell into the silence like a grenade in a glasshouse.

She saw the flash of shock in his face. His eyes flared and he even seemed to jolt backwards as if the words had almost rocked him off his feet.

'Pregnant?' His voice came out hoarsely. 'How can you possibly be pregnant? You've been on the Pill for the whole time we've been together.' He cocked his head accusingly. 'Haven't you?'

Emelia wrung her hands, deciding there was no point in pretending she was invincible any longer. 'I was sick about a month or so ago. I didn't tell you. I had some sort of stomach upset. I think that would have been enough to cancel out the Pill.'

His rough expletive made Emelia flinch. He turned away from her and rubbed a hand over his face. Then he paced the floor a couple of times, back and forth like a caged lion, his jaw pushed all the way forward with tension.

'Don't dare to mention a termination,' she said. 'I won't agree to it and you can't force me.'

He stopped pacing to look at her. 'I do have some measure of humanity about me, Emelia. This is not the child's fault.'

She gave him an accusing glare. 'Are you saying it's *my* fault?'

He raked his hair with his fingers. 'You should have told me you weren't well. What were you thinking?'

'Being sick doesn't come with the job description of corporate trophy wife,' she threw back. 'I'm supposed to be glamorous and perfectly groomed and ready for you at the click of your fingers, remember?'

He stood staring at her, as if seeing her for the first time. 'You think that is what I always expected of you?'

'Wasn't it?' she asked with an embittered look.

He swallowed tightly and sent his hand back through his hair. 'You have it so wrong, Emelia.'

'I know you probably won't believe me, but this is not something I planned,' she said. 'Not like this. I wanted to have a baby but I wanted us to both want it.'

He was so silent she started to feel uncomfortable, wondering if his mind was taking him back to what the press had speciously claimed about her relationship with Peter Marshall.

'This baby is yours, Javier,' she said, holding his gaze. 'You have to believe me on this. There has been no one but you.'

'No one else is going to believe that,' he said, pacing again.

Emelia flattened her mouth. 'So that's what's important to you, is it? What other people think? You didn't seem to mind what people thought when that nightclub singer draped herself all over you.'

He frowned darkly as he turned back to face her. 'Emelia, this is not helping. We have to deal with this.'

'*You* have to deal with it,' she said. 'I have already dealt with it. I want this baby more than anything. It's a miracle to me that it's happened.'

'How many weeks are you?'

'I'm not sure,' she said. 'The doctor thinks only a month, if that.'

He gave a humourless laugh, shaking his head in disbelief. '*Dios mio*, what a mess.'

'This is a child we are talking about,' Emelia said, feeling a little too close to tears than she would have liked. 'I don't consider him or her to be a mess or a problem that has to be solved. I want this baby. I will love it, no matter how or why or when it was conceived.'

Javier saw the shimmering moisture in her eyes and felt a hand grab at his insides. Her hormones were no doubt all over the place and he wasn't helping things by reacting on impulse instead of thinking before he spoke. No wonder she had been so het up about his regular trips to Moscow, especially when that ridiculous article came out on his return. 'Emelia, we'll deal with it,' he said. 'I will support you. You have no need to worry about that. You and the baby will want for nothing.'

She looked at him with wariness in her grey-blue gaze. 'I'm not sure I want my child to grow up with a parental relationship that is not loving and secure.'

He came over and unpeeled her hands from around her body, holding them in the firm grasp of his. 'There are not many things you can bank on in life, Emelia. But I can guarantee you this—whatever happens between us will not affect our child. I won't allow it. We will have to put our issues aside. They can never have priority over the well-being of our child.'

Her expression was still guarded. 'You're not ruling out divorce at some stage, though, are you?'

He drew in a breath, holding it for a beat or two before releasing it. 'There is no reason why a divorce cannot be an amicable arrangement,' he said. 'If we feel the attraction that brought us together is over, I see no reason not to move on with our lives as long as it doesn't cause upset to our child.'

She pulled out of his hold and hugged herself again. 'We clearly don't share the same views on marriage,' she said. 'I've always believed it should be for life. I know things can go wrong but that's true of every relationship, not just a marital one. Surely two sensible adults who respect each other can work their way through a rough patch instead of bailing out in defeat.'

'I find it intriguing that you are suddenly an expert on marriage when you were the one to leave the marital home, not me,' Javier said. 'You pulled the plug, remember?'

Her mouth was pulled so tight it went white at the edges. 'That is so like you, to put the blame back on my shoulders, absolving yourself of any culpability. You drove me from you, Javier. You had no time for me. I was just a toy you picked up and put down at your leisure. I had no assurances from you. I didn't know from one day to the next whether you would be called away on business. Business always came first with you. I gave up everything to be with you, and yet you didn't give me anything in return.'

'I beg to differ, *cariño*,' he said. 'I spent a fortune on clothes and jewellery for you. Every trip I returned from, I gave you a present of some sort. I know many women who would give anything to be in your position.'

She glared at him hotly. 'You just don't get it, do you? I don't want expensive jewellery and designer clothes. I hate those clothes and ridiculous shoes upstairs. They make me feel like a tart. I've never wanted any of that from you.'

'Then, for God's sake, what do you want?' he asked, goaded into raising his voice.

She looked at him bleakly. 'I just want to be loved,' she said so softly he had to strain his ears to hear it. 'I have dreamed of it for so long. My father couldn't do it without conditions. I thought when I met you it would be different, but it wasn't. You want something I can't give you, Javier. I can't be a trophy wife. I can't be a shell of a person. I have to love with my whole being. I gave you my heart and soul and you've crushed it beneath the heel of your cynicism.'

Javier watched as she turned and left the room. She didn't slam the door, as many women would have done. She closed it with a soft little click that ricocheted through him like a gunshot.

CHAPTER TEN

ALMOST a week went past and Emelia saw very little of Javier over that time. He hadn't even come to bed each night until the early hours of the morning, which made her wonder if he was avoiding talking to her. He seemed to be throwing himself into his work until he fell into bed exhausted. Even in sleep she could see the lines of strain around his mouth, and on the rare occasions when his eyes met hers during waking hours they had a haunted shadowed look.

Aldana had come across Emelia being sick a couple of mornings ago as she'd come into the master suite to change the bedlinen. The housekeeper's dark gaze seemed to put two and two together for she said, 'Is that why you came back to Señor Mélendez—because you need a father for your bastard child?'

Emelia straightened her shoulders and met the housekeeper's derisive gaze head on. 'I have tried my best to get on with you. I know you don't think I am good enough for Javier. But if you wish to keep your job, Aldana, I think you should in future keep your opinions to yourself.'

Aldana mumbled something under her breath as she

bundled the rest of the linen in her arms on her way out of the bedroom.

Emelia had put the incident out of her mind but when Javier came home from a trip to Cadiz on Friday evening she could tell something was wrong. She came into the sitting room to see him with a glass of spirits in his hand and it apparently wasn't his first. His mouth was drawn and his eyes were even more shadowed than days before. She could see the tension in his body, his shoulders were slightly hunched and his tie was askew and his shirt crumpled.

'Did you have a hard day?' she asked.

'You could say that.' He took another deep swallow of his drink. 'How about you?'

She sat on the edge of one of the sofas. 'It was OK, I guess. I went for a long ride on Callida.'

'Is that wise?' he asked, frowning at her. 'What if you fell off?'

'I didn't fall off and I will only ride until the doctor says it's time to stop.'

There was a long silence.

'Is something wrong, Javier?' she asked.

He gave her a brooding look. 'Have you spoken to anyone about your pregnancy? I mean outside the villa. A friend or acquaintance or anyone?'

She frowned at him. 'No, of course not. Who would I speak to? I've been stuck here for days on end with nothing better to do than lounge about the pool or ride around in circles while you're off doing God knows what without telling me when you'll be back.'

He moved across to the coffee table and picked up a collection of newspapers. He spread them out before her, his expression dark with fury. 'Have a look at these,' he said. 'You don't need to read them all. Each one of them says the same. *Mélendez Reunion—Love-Child Scandal.*'

Emelia felt her heart slip sideways in her chest. She clutched at her throat as she looked down at the damning words. 'I don't…I don't understand…' She looked up at him in bewilderment. 'How would anyone find out I was pregnant? The doctor wouldn't have said anything. It would be a breach of patient confidentiality.'

In one sweep of his hand he shoved the papers off onto the floor. 'This is exactly what I wanted to avoid,' he said, scowling in anger.

Emelia moistened her bone-dry lips. 'I exchanged a few words with Aldana the other day,' she said. 'I was going to mention it to you but you were late getting back.'

His gaze cut to hers. 'What did you say?'

'It was more what she said to me,' she said. 'She was in our room changing the bed when she heard me being sick. When I came out she accused me of only coming back to you because…because I needed a father for my child.'

His brow was like a map of lines. 'What did you say to her in response?'

Emelia elevated her chin. 'I told her she should keep her opinions to herself if she wanted to continue working here.'

A dark cloud drifted over his features. 'I see.'

'She's never liked me, Javier,' she said. 'You know yourself she's never really accepted me as your wife. She won't let me do anything or touch anything or bring anything into this stupid over-decorated, too formal mausoleum. I've tried to be polite to her but I can't allow her to say such an insulting thing to me.'

'I understand completely,' he said. 'I will have a word with her.'

'You don't have to fire her on my account,' she said, looking down at her hands. 'It might not have been her, in any case…I mean, leaking the news of my pregnancy to the press.'

Javier came over to her and placed one of his hands on her shoulder. 'You are prepared to give her the benefit of the doubt when everything points to her being guilty?'

She looked up at him. 'But of course. She's never spoken to the press before. She loves working for you. It's her whole life, managing the villa. I don't think she would deliberately jeopardise that.'

He placed his fingers beneath her chin, his thumb moving over the fullness of her bottom lip. 'You are far too trusting, *querida*,' he said. 'People often have nefarious motives for what they do, even the people you care about.'

'That stuff in the paper…' She glanced down at the scattered mess on the floor. 'Is there nothing we can do?'

He pulled her gently to her feet, holding her about the waist. 'Don't worry about it,' he said. 'It will blow over eventually.'

She looked into his eyes. 'Javier… You really believe this baby is yours, don't you?'

Javier realised she was asking much more than that. She was asking for a commitment from him that he had never wanted to give before. He wasn't sure he wanted to give it even now. How could he be sure he wouldn't turn out like his father? But what he had begun to realise over the past few days was that being a father was not just a biological contribution. It was a contract of love and commitment with no conditions attached. His father had not been capable of going that step further. He had impregnated his mother but once she had died he had not fulfilled his responsibilities as a father. He had shunted Javier off to teachers and nannies while he'd got on with his life. This baby Emelia was carrying deserved to be loved and cherished and he was going to make sure it lacked for nothing. 'The baby is ours,' he said watching as her eyes shone with tears. 'I am proud to be its father.'

'I love you,' she said as she wrapped her arms around him tightly.

He rested his chin on the top of her head and held her close. 'I'm very glad that is one thing you remembered,' he said.

She looked up from his chest and smiled. 'I would have fallen in love with you all over again if I hadn't.'

'You think so?'

'I know so,' she said and reached up to meet his descending mouth.

Paris was enjoying an Indian summer and each day seemed brighter and warmer than the previous one. The first week they had spent wandering around the Louvre and Notre Dame, stopping for coffee in one of the numerous cafés. They had mostly been able to avoid the paparazzi, although one particularly determined journalist had followed them all the way up the Eiffel Tower steps for an impromptu interview. Javier had been extremely protective of Emelia, holding her close against his body as he'd curtly told the reporter to leave them alone. It had made Emelia glow inside to think of him standing up for her like that. It made her wonder if he was in love with her after all. She sometimes caught him looking at her with a thoughtful expression on his face, as if he was seeing her with new eyes.

The hotel Javier had booked them into was luxurious and private and close to all the sights. He even organised a private tour of the Palace of Versailles, outside of Paris, which meant she didn't have to be jostled by crowds of tourists.

They were walking past the fountain towards the woodland area when Emelia felt the first cramp. She had been feeling a little out of sorts since the night before but had put it down to the rich meal they had eaten in one of Paris's premier restaurants.

Javier noticed her slight stumble and put his arm around her waist. 'Steady there, *cariño*,' he said. 'You don't want to take a fall.'

She smiled weakly and settled against his hold, walking a few more paces when another pain gripped her like a large fish hook. She placed a hand against her abdomen, her skin breaking out in clamminess.

'Emelia?' Javier stopped and gripped her by both arms. 'What's wrong?'

She bit down on her lip as another cramp clawed at her. 'I think something's wrong…I'm having cramps. Oh, God…' Her legs began to fold but he caught her just in time.

He scooped her up in his arms and walked briskly to the nearest guide, who promptly called an ambulance.

Emelia remembered the pain and the ashen features of Javier as she was loaded into the back of the ambulance and then nothing…

* * *

When she woke the first thing Emelia saw was Javier sitting asleep in the chair beside her bed. He jolted awake as if he had sensed her looking at him. Relief flooded his features as he grasped her hand and entwined his fingers with hers. 'You gave me such a fright, *querida*. I thought I was going to lose you all over again. You have taken ten years off my life, I am sure.'

Emelia dreaded asking, but did so all the same. 'The baby?'

He shook his head. 'I'm sorry, *mi amor*. They couldn't prevent the miscarriage but you are safe, that is the main thing.'

Emelia felt her hopes plummet. The main thing was he was off the hook, surely? No more baby. No more commitment. No more pretending to be happy about being a father. 'How far along was I?' she asked in an expressionless tone.

'Not long, just a month, I think I heard one of the doctors say.'

Emelia studied his expression without saying anything.

He shifted in his seat, his eyes going to their joined hands. 'I know what you are thinking, Emelia,' he said gruffly. 'And I know I deserve it for how I reacted to the news of the pregnancy. I didn't exactly embrace the idea with any enthusiasm.'

'I'd like to be alone for a while,' she said.

He looked at her again. 'But we need to talk about the future.'

She pulled her hand away and stuffed it under the sheets. 'I don't want to talk right now.'

He slowly rose to his feet as if his bones ached like those of an old man. 'I'll be waiting outside.'

Emelia held off the tears until he had left but once

the door closed on the private room she let them fall. So he wanted to talk about the future, did he? What future was that? She had been lulled into thinking they could make a go of their marriage but he had not once told her he loved her. He always held something of himself back. She was never going to be able to penetrate the fortress of his heart. Not now, not without the baby she had longed for, the baby she had hoped would be the key to showing him the meaning of love. She had seen the flicker of relief in his eyes. No pregnancy meant he could continue with his life the way he always had—free and unfettered. Well, he was going to be much more free and unfettered than he bargained for, she decided.

'How is she?' Javier asked the doctor on duty when he came back from the bathroom.

'She doesn't want to see anyone right now,' the doctor said. 'She is still feeling rather low. It's quite normal, of course. The disruption of hormones takes its toll. She can go on some antidepressants if she doesn't improve.'

'When can I take her home?'

'She lost a lot of blood,' the doctor said. 'She's had a transfusion so we'd like her to stay in for a few days to build up her strength. She has been through rather a lot just lately, I see from the notes.'

'Yes,' Javier said, feeling guilt like a scratchy yoke about his shoulders. 'Yes, she has.'

'Just be patient,' the doctor advised. 'There's no reason why she can't conceive again. These things happen. Sometimes it's just nature's way of saying the time is not right.'

Javier sighed as the doctor moved on down the

corridor. He had never thought there would be a right time, and yet the right time had come and gone and he had not even realised it.

The nurse handed Emelia her discharge form with a disapproving frown. 'The doctor is not happy about you wanting to leave so soon, especially without your husband with you. Can't you wait until he gets here? He's probably stuck in traffic. There was an accident in one of the tunnels this morning.'

Emelia straightened her shoulders. 'I have been here for four days as it is. I am sick of being fussed over. I am sick of hospitals. I want to get on with my life.'

'But your husband—'

'Will understand completely when he hears I have left,' Emelia said with a jut of her chin as she picked up her bag. 'You can tell him goodbye for me.'

Emelia slipped out of the hospital, keeping her head down in case anyone recognised her. The press had been lurking about, or so one of the cleaning staff had informed her. That had made her decision a lot easier to make. She was tired of living in a fish bowl. She was tired of being someone she wasn't, someone she had never been and never could be. The accident had been devastating but it hadn't been the catalyst everyone assumed it had been. She had already made up her mind that she could no longer live the life Javier had planned for them both. It didn't matter what his reasons were for marrying her, the fact remained that he didn't love her. He wasn't capable of loving anyone. And, while she loved him and would love him for the rest of her life, she could not continue living in hope that he would change.

A taxi pulled into the entrance of the hospital and,

once its occupants had settled up, Emelia got in and directed the driver to the airport. She had already booked the flight via the high tech mobile phone Javier had brought in for her. It was another one of his expensive presents, one of many he had brought in over the last few days: a pair of diamond earrings and a matching pendant, a bottle of perfume, a designer watch that looked more like a bracelet than a timepiece, and some slips of lace that were supposed to be underwear. She had received them all with a tight little smile, her heart breaking into little pieces for the one gift he withheld—his love.

The flight was on time, which meant Emelia could finally let out her breath once she was strapped into the seat, ready for take-off. She checked the watch Javier had given her, her fingers tracing over the tiny sparkling diamonds embedded around the face as she thought about him arriving right about now on the ward. He would be demanding to know where she was, where she had gone and who she had gone with. She could almost see his thunderous expression, his tightly clenched hands and the deep lines scoring his forehead. But, for some reason, instead of making her smile in satisfaction, she buried her head in her hands and wept.

CHAPTER ELEVEN

EMELIA had spent the afternoon on the beach. The walk back to her father's palatial holiday house at Sunshine Beach in Queensland was her daily exercise. It still felt strange to be on speaking terms with her father after all this time. But his recent health scare had made him take stock of his life and he had gone out of his way since she had returned to make up for the past. He had given her the house to use for as long as she wanted. He flew up on occasional weekends when he could get away from work and she enjoyed their developing relationship, even though they didn't always see eye to eye on everything. Emelia had even made a fragile sort of peace with his young wife who, she realised, really did love her father in spite of his many faults. In many ways Krystal reminded her of herself when she had met and married Javier. Krystal was a little naïve and star-struck by the world her husband lived in and did everything she could to please him. It made Emelia cringe to witness it, but she knew there was nothing she could say.

The one thing Emelia and her father crossed swords over was Javier. Her father thought she shouldn't have run away without speaking to him. In Michael Shelverton's opinion, sending Javier divorce papers three weeks after she had left was a coward's way out. He felt she should have at least given him a hearing.

Emelia was glad she had done things the way she had. She wanted a clean break to allow herself time to heal. But after a month she still had trouble sleeping in spite of the hours of walking and swimming she did each day to bring on the mindless exhaustion she craved.

She had covered her tracks as best she could to avoid Javier finding her. She'd gone back to her maiden name and only answered the phone if she recognised the number on the caller ID device. She had also organised with her father to have all mail go via his post office box address and he then forwarded it on to her.

She tried not to think about Javier but it was impossible to rid her memory of his touch. Her body ached for him night after night and sometimes when she was half-asleep she found herself reaching into the empty space beside her in the bed in the vain hope of finding him there.

Emelia came up the path to the front door of the house with keys in hand, but stopped dead when a tall figure rose from the wrought iron seat on the deck.

'Hello, Emelia,' Javier said.

She set her mouth and moved past him to open the door. 'You had better leave before I call the police,' she said, stabbing the keys into the lock.

He stepped closer. 'We need to talk.'

She tried not to shrink away from his towering presence. 'You can say whatever you want to say via my lawyer.'

'That is not the way I do things, Emelia, or at least not this time around. I made that mistake before. I won't be making it again. This time it is face to face until we work this out.'

Emelia tried to block him from following her inside but he put one foot inside the door. 'If you don't want to be visiting a podiatrist for the rest of your life, I suggest you take your foot out the doorway.'

He took hold of the door, his eyes challenging hers in a heated duel she knew she would never win. 'We can discuss this out here or we can discuss it inside,' he said in an implacable tone. 'I am not leaving until this is sorted out, one way or the other.'

Emelia let the door go and stalked inside. She tossed her beach bag on the floor of the marbled foyer and, hands on hips, faced him. 'How did you find me?' she asked.

'Your father gave me the address.'

Her eyes flared with outrage. *'My father?'* She clenched her hands into fists. 'Why, that double-crossing, lying cheat. I knew I shouldn't have fallen for that stupid father-daughter reunion thing. I should have known he would take sides with you. What a jerk.'

'He loves you, Emelia,' Javier said. 'He's always loved you but he's not good at showing it, much less saying it.'

Her hands went to her hips again. 'So now you're the big expert on relationships,' she said. 'Well, bully for you.'

'He wants you to be happy.'

'I'm perfectly happy.' She put up her chin. 'In fact, I've never been happier.'

'You look tired and far too thin.'

She rolled her eyes. 'You're not looking so hot yourself, big guy.'

'That's because I can't sleep without you.'

Something flickered in her eyes. 'I'm sure you will find someone to take my place, if you haven't already.'

He shook his head at her. 'You don't get it, do you?'

She stood her ground, reminding him of a small terrier in a stand-off with a Rottweiler. 'What am I supposed to get? I understand why you married me, Javier. I've always understood. I was an idiot to agree to it, but that's what people who are blinded by love do, stupid, stupid things. But things are different now. I left you before but the accident put things on hold. This time I am determined to go through with it. It's over, Javier. Our marriage is over.'

Javier swallowed the restriction in his throat. 'I don't want a divorce.'

She visibly stiffened. 'What did you say?'

'You heard me, *querida*.'

She screwed up her face in a scowl. 'Don't call me that.'

'*Mi amor.*'

Her eyes flashed at him angrily. 'That's an even bigger lie. I am not your love. I have never been and never will be. I can handle it, you know. I get it, *finally*. Some men just can't love another person. They hate being vulnerable. It's the way they are wired. It can't be changed.'

'On the contrary, I think it can be changed,' Javier said. '*I* have changed. I am prepared to let myself be vulnerable. I love you so much but I refused to admit it before in case it was snatched away from me. I have been lying to myself for all this time. Well, maybe not lying—more protecting myself, just as you described. I have always held something back in case I was let down.'

She stood so still and so silent, as if she had stopped breathing.

He took a breath and continued. 'I think I have always loved you, the *real* you, Emelia. You don't have to be stick-thin and done up like a supermodel to make my heart leap in my throat. You do that just by waking up beside me with pillow creases on your cheeks and blurry eyes and fighting off a cold.'

Emelia swallowed. Was she dreaming? Was she hearing what she wanted to hear instead of what he was actually saying? That happened sometimes. She had heard of it. She had done it herself, talked herself into thinking she had heard things, just because she hoped and hoped and hoped someone would say them...

'I have shut off my emotions for most of my life,' he said. 'Saying *I love you* is something I saw as a weakness. I guess I have seen any vulnerability as a weakness. That is probably why you felt you couldn't tell me when you weren't feeling well. I blame myself for that. I should have known. I should have looked out for you. Even Izabella has pointed it out to me, how closed off I am.'

'I'm not sure what this has to do with me now...' she said uncertainly.

'It has everything to do with you, *cariño*,' he said softly. 'I have loved you from the first moment you smiled at me. I can even remember the day. It was our first date. Do you remember it? Please tell me you haven't forgotten it. I would hate for you not to remember the one moment that has defined my life from then on.'

Emelia gave a small nod, her breath still locked in her throat. 'I remember.'

'You looked at me across the table at that restaurant and smiled at something I said. It was like an arrow had pierced my heart, just like Cupid's bow. I didn't know what had hit me. I hated feeling so out of control.'

She summoned up a frown, not quite willing to let go just yet. 'Your father's will,' she said. 'You can't deny that it had something to do with why we married in such a rush. You should have told me about it from the start. Finding out the way I did really hurt me. I felt so used.'

He pushed his hand through his hair. 'I didn't even know about my father's will until I had been seeing you for over a month. I had never considered myself the marrying kind. I had seen the way my father had ruined three women's lives. I didn't want to do that. I guess that's why he wrote his will that way. It was just the sort of sick joke he would have liked—to force me to do something I didn't want to do. Prior to being involved with you, I had always kept all of my relationships on a casual basis.'

His expression twisted with remorse as he continued. 'I should have told you everything about that damned will. Instead, I let Claudine get her claws in. The thing is, I didn't want my father's money for myself. I wanted Izabella to have what was rightly hers and I didn't want to lose you. Marriage seemed a good way of keeping both things secure.'

She still looked at him doubtfully. 'I don't think I can cope with living at the villa any longer. I know it's beautiful and grand and all that but it's way too formal for me. I feel like I am going to get roused on for bumping into things or if something breaks.'

He came over to where she was standing, stopping just in front of her. 'The villa needs to be a home instead of a showpiece,' he said. 'I can see that now. No wonder you never felt at ease there. That is another thing I should have realised. It needs a woman's touch—your touch—to make it the home it should always have been. Aldana has decided to retire. I have been a fool not to realise how difficult she made things for you. She didn't speak to the press—apparently, that was one of the junior gardeners—but she told me about the roses. She feels very remorseful about how she treated you. I should have told you myself why I hate having them in the house.'

She looked at him with a searching gaze. 'Did I know that before the accident?'

He brushed his fingertips over the gentle slope of her cheek. 'No,' he said. 'That was another vulnerability I didn't allow you to see. They remind me of my mother's funeral. Red ones are the worst. I can't bear the sight of them. I would have had every rose bush at the villa dug up and burned by now but my mother had planted them herself.'

Emelia felt the ice around her heart begin to crack. 'I didn't really want to leave you, Javier. I just felt I had no choice. And then the accident...' She gulped and continued hollowly, 'Maybe Peter would still be alive if it hadn't been for me.'

He gripped her hands. 'No, you must not think like that. I have heard from the police since you left. The accident was no accident. Peter's lover was being stalked by her ex. He was following you and Peter, mistakenly believing you to be her. He ran Peter off the road. Charges are in the process of being laid. You were not at fault.'

She put a hand to her head and frowned as the memory returned. 'I remember Vanessa. She was the best thing that had ever happened to Peter. They were so in love.'

He gave her a pained look. 'I know. I am ashamed of how I reacted to that ridiculous press story. I should have trusted you. You've had to endure similar rubbish and yet you've always trusted me.'

'Until that last time,' she said. 'The Russian singer.'

'Yes, well, that was perfectly understandable,' he said. 'You were in the early stages of pregnancy. I had never made you feel all that secure in our marriage. I was always flying off to sign up some big business deal. But all that has to change—if you'll only give me a chance.' He tightened his hold of her hands. 'Say you'll come back to me, Emelia. Come back to me and be my wife. Be the mother of my children.'

Emelia blinked back tears. 'We lost our little baby…'

He pulled her into his chest. 'I know,' he said, softly planting a kiss on the top of her head, her seawater-damp and salty hair tickling his nose. 'I blame myself for that. If you hadn't been so worried about me coming to terms with being a father, maybe it wouldn't have happened.'

She pulled back in his embrace to look up at him. 'You mustn't blame yourself. My father recently told me my mother had three miscarriages before she had me. I don't know if it's hereditary or not, but I'm sure we'll have a baby one day.'

'So you'll come back to me?' he asked.

She smiled as she linked her arms around his neck. 'I can't think of any place I would rather be than with you.'

His dark eyes melted as he looked down at her. 'I know someone who is going to be absolutely thrilled to hear you say that.'

She gave him a quizzical look. 'Who?'

'She's waiting in the car,' he said. 'She said something about BFF. What does that mean, by the way?'

Emelia's smile widened. 'It means best friends forever. She's really here? Izabella came all this way?'

His smile was self-deprecating. 'She didn't trust me to be able to convince you to come home. She said if I didn't succeed she would come in and do it for me. Do you want me to call her in?'

'Of course I do.' She ran to the window and, finding the hire car, waved madly to the young woman sitting inside chewing her nails.

Javier's gaze warmed as he came over and looped an arm around her waist. 'There's just one thing I need to do before she gets here,' he said, turning her around to face him.

'Oh,' Emelia said, smiling brightly. 'What's that?'

'I think you know,' he said and, before she could admit she did, he covered her mouth with a kiss that promised forever.

MILLS & BOON
MODERN™

The Drakos Baby

An enthralling linked-story duet by best-selling author

LYNNE GRAHAM

A Greek billionaire with amnesia, a secret baby, a convenient marriage…it's a recipe for rip-roaring passion, revelations and the reunion of a lifetime!

PART ONE
THE PREGNANCY SHOCK
On sale 16th July

Billie is PA to gorgeous Greek billionaire Alexei Drakos. After just one magical night together, an accident leaves Alexei with amnesia and Billie discovers she's pregnant – *by a man who has no recollection of having slept with her…*

PART TWO
A STORMY GREEK MARRIAGE
On sale 20th August

Billie's baby has been born but she hasn't told Alexei about his son's existence. But her return to Greece and their marriage of convenience will lead to a shocking revelation for Alexei…

MILLS & BOON

are proud to present our...

Book of the Month

Time Raiders:
The Protector
by Merline Lovelace
from Mills & Boon®
Nocturne™

Cassandra's psychic skills are the reason she's
been sent to seventh-century China on a
dangerous mission. Soldier Max is supposed
to protect her, but when the crusade turns
deadly, Max and Cassie are powerless to
fight their growing attraction.

Mills & Boon® Nocturne™
Available 18th June

*Something to say about our
Book of the Month?
Tell us what you think!*
millsandboon.co.uk/community

2 FREE BOOKS
AND A SURPRISE GIFT

We would like to take this opportunity to thank you for reading this Mills & Boon® book by offering you the chance to take TWO more specially selected books from the Modern™ series absolutely FREE! We're also making this offer to introduce you to the benefits of the Mills & Boon® Book Club™—

- **FREE home delivery**
- **FREE gifts and competitions**
- **FREE monthly Newsletter**
- **Exclusive Mills & Boon Book Club offers**
- **Books available before they're in the shops**

Accepting these FREE books and gift places you under no obligation to buy, you may cancel at any time, even after receiving your free books. Simply complete your details below and return the entire page to the address below. You don't even need a stamp!

YES Please send me 2 free Modern books and a surprise gift. I understand that unless you hear from me, I will receive 4 superb new books every month for just £3.19 each, postage and packing free. I am under no obligation to purchase any books and may cancel my subscription at any time. The free books and gift will be mine to keep in any case.

Ms/Mrs/Miss/Mr _____ Initials _____

Surname _____

Address _____

_____

_____ Postcode _____

E-mail _____

Send this whole page to: Mills & Boon Book Club, Free Book Offer, FREEPOST NAT 10298, Richmond, TW9 1BR

Offer valid in UK only and is not available to current Mills & Boon Book Club subscribers to this series. Overseas and Eire please write for details.. We reserve the right to refuse an application and applicants must be aged 18 years or over. Only one application per household. Terms and prices subject to change without notice. Offer expires 30th June 2010. As a result of this application, you may receive offers from Harlequin Mills & Boon and other carefully selected companies. If you would prefer not to share in this opportunity please write to The Data Manager, PO Box 676, Richmond, TW9 1WU.

Mills & Boon® is a registered trademark owned by Harlequin Mills & Boon Limited. Modern™ is being used as a trademark. The Mills & Boon® Book Club™ is being used as a trademark.